He saw something in her eyes.

So different than when she'd been young. When touching had been easy and natural and they'd been crazy about each other. Now she was Meg, the cop. Meg, the woman he barely recognized.

"It's been a long time since…"

Since they stood within each other's proximity. Since they talked, actually talked.

What do you want me to say, Meggie? That I haven't forgotten what we had once?

"How've you been?" she asked softly.

His heart hammered. Well, it was a start....

Dear Reader,

More and more frequently we hear about bullying in schools. Children are hurt emotionally, physically, spiritually. As a teacher, I've seen the results bullying can inflict on a child's esteem. The emotional scars can run so deep they remain visible in adulthood. Other times, those same scars can create a courage and inner strength few people understand.

When I wrote *The Man from Montana* (December 2006) and introduced Ethan Red Wolf, I realized I'd come upon a man who had endured bullying as a child—and triumphed. Now Ethan's strong yet gentle heart must help the woman he has loved all his life overcome the heartache of *her* past. I hope you enjoy their road to happiness as much as I enjoyed creating it.

I love hearing from my readers, so if you'd like to drop me a line I can be contacted at www.maryjforbes.com.

Warm wishes,

Mary

RED WOLF'S RETURN

MARY J. FORBES

SPECIAL EDITION

Published by Silhouette Books

America's Publisher of Contemporary Romance

SILHOUETTE BOOKS

ISBN-13: 978-0-373-24858-2
ISBN-10:   0-373-24858-X

RED WOLF'S RETURN

Books by Mary J. Forbes

Silhouette Special Edition

A Forever Family #1625
A Father, Again #1661
Everything She's Ever Wanted #1702
Twice Her Husband #1755
The Man from Montana #1800
His Brother's Gift #1840
Red Wolf's Return #1858

MARY J. FORBES

grew up on a farm amid horses, cattle, crisp hay and broad blue skies. As a child, she drew and wrote of her surroundings, and in sixth grade composed her first story about a little lame pony. Years later, she worked as an accountant, then as a reporter-photographer for a small-town newspaper, before earning an honors degree in education to become a teacher. She has also written and published short fiction stories.

A romantic by nature, Mary loves walking along the ocean shoreline, sitting by the fire on snowy or rainy evenings and two-stepping around the dance floor to a good country song—all with her own real-life hero, of course. Mary would love to hear from her readers at www.maryjforbes.com.

For G—always

Chapter One

A mist lay on the lagoon below Blue Mountain the September morning Ethan Red Wolf faced a past he'd buried years ago.

Won't be hi and bye this time, Meggie.

No, he'd have to make an elaborate report of the wounded eagle huddling against the boulder. Which meant talking to *her.*

"Easy," he soothed when the raptor squirmed weakly on the shoreline rocks. Slipping his Nikon camera into his backpack, he crouched for closer inspection—and mentally cursed.

The bird's tail feathers had been plucked like unwanted hairs.

Thankfully, the cool, rainy temperatures during the past two days had kept the scent down and coyotes and wolves at bay—a cleanup process as old as the mountain above him.

He snorted softly. Wasn't this just bloody typical? Seemed after all these years, America's heritage symbol—*his* heritage symbol—would be the catalyst bringing him eye to eye with Sweet Creek's police chief.

Meggie McKee.

Gently he lifted the bird. "It's gonna be okay, little lady," he murmured. Rising, he cradled the eagle against his chest before starting over the rocks toward his house on the other side of the diminutive lake shrouded in the foggy dawn.

Ah, Meggie, he thought. *We're about to have a real conversation.* A first since she'd returned to Montana from the west coast six years ago.

Hell, if he were honest with himself, this would the first time they exchanged more than ten words in nineteen years.

Sure, they had nodded to each other on the street, said "Hi" in passing, had even traded the old, "How's it going?" "Oh, fine. You?" "Good, good…" when he used to work as her brother's foreman on the Flying Bar T Ranch.

But a conversation? An honest-to-God, intelligent discourse between two people?

Every time they were within ten feet of each other, one or other zipped to an exit at the first chance. Him, because of her marriage—and too many other reasons he'd locked away over the years. Her…well, her reason had been the one he'd never forgotten. The one she had decided the night of their prom. *You're not what I want in a man, after all.*

Today, another female would alter fate. He looked down at the eagle with her shot-up wing and thigh and shook his head. *Little lady…if you only knew what your sacrifice is about to set in motion.*

Because he sure as hell wasn't talking to Gilby Pierce, Meggie's second-in-command. Nope, Ethan intended to speak to the head gal herself—if for no other reason than to establish some prolonged face time.

He walked through the thick timber and across a minimeadow where two hours ago his camera lens had caught the chipmunk chewing a seed on the rotted log. At the crest of a small knoll, he appraised the little homestead his grandfather Davis O'Conner had built a half century before. Protected by a grove of pine, aspen and birch, rich in autumn splendor, the renovated house sat two hundred yards from the lagoon.

His home now. *His* spot on the map.

He wondered if in the past year—since he'd taken residency on this side of the hill a quarter mile from where Meggie lived with her sixteen-year-old son— had she ever looked down onto his home as he did now?

Don't be a fool, Ethan. She's a different woman than she was at eighteen. All brass and guts now.

She needed to be, as chief of police.

The Meggie he'd kissed as a teenager no longer existed. This Meggie wouldn't spare one frivolous second mooning over some bygone childhood love.

That much he'd witnessed in the past six years after Mayor Hudson Leland and the town council hired her to run Sweet Creek's police department. Hell, not long ago, she'd practiced at the former rifle range—shot bull's-eyes, in fact—an eighth of a mile from Ethan's house. A range on the property left to him by his late grandfather that Ethan had bulldozed last June to make room for the therapeutic riding center he wanted to establish. Which, of course, didn't sit well with the locals, including the mayor and his cronies—in particular Jock Ralston.

Lifting his head, Ethan sought out the mammoth boulder sitting like a rough-edged beacon across the lake. The boulder where he'd found the raptor.

Where, under a stadium of stars, eighteen-year-old Meggie McKee had once said she would love him forever.

Ethan grunted. *Right. And there went a lake of water under that bridge.*

Firmly cradling the bird in his arms, he walked down the hill toward the house in the trees.

A thicket of yellow aspen on the outskirts of town encircled Sweet Creek's animal clinic. Turning into its lane, Ethan squinted as the dawn light glanced off the windshield of the doctor's van in front of the tomato-red barn.

Three minutes later, after carrying the injured eagle into the reception area, he and his longtime friend and town veterinarian, Kell Tanner, considered the bird's wounds on an examination table.

"Can you save her, Doc?" Ethan wanted to know.

"It'll be touch-and-go. Only blessing is she has youth on her side." He removed the tea towels Ethan had bound around the wings. Before bringing the bird in, he'd dribbled water into its beak with an eyedropper until its glassy yellow eyes blinked open, the nictitating membranes gliding slowly across the corneas, back to front. At that point, Ethan had breathed a sigh of hope.

Gently the veterinarian carefully probed the bird's torn thigh and shattered wing. "Damn shame."

And then some. "Do your best, Doc. She deserves it."

Kell nodded. "Come back in a couple hours. She'll be in recovery then."

"Thanks." Ethan headed for the door.

"You realize they're not going to like what you're thinking here," Kell said over his shoulder. "That one of their gun buddies might be a poacher."

They. The law or the town council? Ethan shrugged. "Guess I'll take the chance."

"Good luck."

Ethan nodded.

Outside, mellow morning sunshine warmed his face as he looked toward the trees across the road separating the clinic from the town proper where two blocks away he'd noticed her pickup at the police station's curb. *Still the early riser, Meggie?*

He pulled his ball cap from a hip pocket, settled it on his head.

Time to get the show on the road.

Resolute, he climbed into his pickup and pulled out of the clinic's graveled parking lot. In the two minutes it took to get to the station, he thought about how she would react to his information, facts that would likely separate them further if he implicated the gun club. *Or her son.* Well, if that was how it played out he'd take the chance anyway. This was for the raptor.

Besides, Meggie lived her own life now—though he'd observed her hire on as chief, watched her son, Beau, grow from a kid with freckles to a teenager with a bad-boy attitude.

Like you were at that age.

And he had watched Meggie date other men, even get serious about one four years ago.

Not that there hadn't been women in Ethan's life.

He'd had his share and then some. Except none had ever measured up to dark-haired, blue-eyed, long-legged Chief Meggie.

Meg. That's the name she used these days. Meg. Hard and headstrong. *Huh.* Well, she'd always be Meg*gie* to him. Soft and sweet natured. The girl he remembered.

Heart pounding, he parked in front of the rectangular wooden structure that had been the police station for nearly two and half decades. Moments later he pulled open its door to walk into a room that took up most of the front length of the building. LED day lighting presented the brightness of July at noon.

She stood to the right, viewing a county map tacked to the wall with her second-in-command Gilby Pierce and dispatcher/secretary Sally Dunn. All three turned, pinning Ethan like the map they'd been scrutinizing.

Meggie's eyes went wide, then she caught herself, and a smile Ethan knew was meant for the sake of her companions curved her mouth before she stepped forward.

For five long seconds he couldn't inhale. *Meggie.*

"Mr. Red Wolf."

Mr. Red Wolf. Fine. She wanted to playact, he'd give her one hell of a performance. "Chief McKee."

Blue uniform crisp, gun slung on her belt, she was all cop in her approach. "Something we can do for you?"

He looked into those beguiling blue eyes. *Well now, Meggie-girl. You're finally looking at me for longer than sixty seconds. How's it feel?*

Hell. He had no delusion that she saw *him;* it was the probable complaint he'd come about that held her interest.

"There is. An eagle's been shot on my property, and I'm wondering if it wasn't for possible profit."

Those fine, black brows he had traced with his mouth twenty years before arced. "Care to explain?"

"Tail and wing feathers missing. Bird's over at Kell's getting its thigh sewn up and its wing bones splinted."

"It's alive?"

"Barely."

She studied him for a moment, assessing his words while he assessed her. Her dark chocolate hair, worn in a neat bob, was shorter than his by several inches. She wore no lipstick, very little rouge, and her gaze was direct in a way it hadn't been when she was a girl. Regret coursed through him at the sight of the hair-fine lines caging those same eyes. She'd had her share of heartache, he surmised. Hell, maybe she still mourned for her ex—the renowned Dr. Doug Sutcliffe—these six years. Ethan shoved away the notion. Meggie thinking about a man bothered him for reasons he did not want to investigate, especially when she was no longer his. *Never had been, Ethan.*

"Why don't you step into my office?" Turning, she led him down a short hallway to a cluttered room with a long wooden desk supporting a computer. Several filing cabinets filled the right wall while the left held another county map, a half-dozen Wanted posters, and a corner window with—irony of ironies—a view of Blue Mountain.

Daily those lake-blue eyes saw the terrain where he lived.

Where *she* lived a shout away.

Did that ever cross her mind?

"Have a seat." All business, she shut the door behind them.

Ethan took the only chair free of file folders. Mere feet from his knees, she hiked a slim hip on her desk and crossed her arms. "Where'd you find the bird?"

"Across the water from my place. On the shore," he added and observed her pinpoint the area in her mind, remembering spots where, as high school sweethearts, they had done their share of kissing.

"Anyone been using the rifle range without your knowledge?" she asked.

"The range doesn't exist anymore, as you know." After the town's rental lease had expired last spring, he'd demolished the target hill and shooting stalls, removed the obstacle course used for the annual Mounted Shoot. He had wanted no part remaining of the thirty-year-old range his grandfather founded. In its place Ethan was creating a healing-horse retreat where troubled kids could find a little peace. Kids like he'd once been.

But his plans were not her affair.

"I'm well aware the range is gone," Meggie replied. "However, that doesn't mean people won't try to use those twenty acres." A corner of her mouth lifted. "Old habits die hard. I was wondering if some folks still consider the field open for target practice."

"I've posted No Trespassing signs." He shifted his booted foot several inches from her police-issued shoe. "But you're right. It doesn't rule out the mayor's gun cronies."

Her gaze didn't waver. "What are you saying, Ethan?"

An air balloon's torch whooshed through him. The last time his name crossed her lips... Hell, he couldn't recall.

"I'm saying I've seen hunters on Blue Mountain."
And one of them was your son.

She slipped off the desk, walked around to her chair.
"Who?" she asked, her fingers easy on the computer's
keyboard. All police business now.

"Couple kids."

Her head swung around. "With rifles?"

"Twenty-twos."

"I need names, Ethan."

Ethan again. Twice in less than sixty seconds. "Randy
Leland, Linc's boy and the mayor's grandson—"

"I know the Lelands," she retorted. Her eyes softened. "Sorry. Didn't mean to snap. It's just… Let's say
it doesn't surprise me."

Of course it didn't. Linc Leland and Jock Ralston—
and sometimes her second-in-command Gilby Pierce—
had blighted Ethan's high school years, and Meggie, his
noble, valiant Meggie, had tried to install herself as his
shield. Until he'd had to physically fight Linc and
Jock—and get his nose busted—to prove himself.

He gave her a half beat. "I also saw your son."

"Beau?" Her pupils pinpricked. "With Randy? When?"

"Last weekend." Labor Day weekend. "Sunday to be
exact. They were popping shots at deadwood on my
land."

She typed in his response. "Did you talk to them?"

He hesitated. Her son hadn't welcomed Ethan's intru-
sion. "I told them to use the range at Livingston or
Bozeman, that they were on private property now." Her
son had shrugged and said something about how Old Man
O'Conner never gave a rat's ass before, why should
Ethan?

He'd told the boy if he didn't get *his* ass off the property right quick, he'd find it hauled down to the chief's office. Or words to that effect. The kid had laughed.

"Did they leave?" Meggie asked.

"They did." Just to be sure, he'd followed them until they were in Beau's Chevy pickup and roaring down the dirt road that wound around the lake and hooked up with the pavement to Sweet Creek's town proper.

"Was that the only time you saw the kids on your land?"

"Beau was there once before, far as I know."

Her expression remained bland. "When?"

"End of July. He was walking along the lakeshore around seven-thirty in the evening."

"With the twenty-two?"

"Over his shoulder."

"Did you talk to him at that time?"

"No. He was crossing my property line and heading up the mountain." Foothill, actually. Blue Mountain was part of the timbered hills evolving into the Absaroka Range to the east.

Meggie got out of her chair and walked to the corner window where the strengthening morning sunlight fell in a block on the floor. Ethan envisioned her conjuring pictures of her boy on the mountain beyond. "Still doesn't mean those kids shot that eagle."

"You're right," he conceded. "It doesn't."

It could have been someone else, an adult, a poacher or poachers trafficking eagle parts. Off and on such stories had been on the nightly news, in the papers. Stories relaying the profit of wildlife products such as bear claws, teeth and gall bladders, antler velvet, hooves from elk and deer.

Of feathers and talons from birds of prey.

Or it could it have been a brash sixteen-year-old proving a point to his mother, officer of the law.

She returned to the desk. "I'll need a statement from you. Please," she added, and again the severity in her eyes lessened. "When Beau gets home from school this afternoon, I'll talk to him."

Ethan didn't envy her the job. He'd heard the rumors, the gossip. Over the past year and a half, Meg McKee's boy had transitioned into the classic bad-assed teenager.

The way he'd been once.

Old history, Ethan.

Except, people didn't forget. Not in this town. Restless to leave, he took the pen and notepad she dug from a desk drawer.

"The room across the hall's more private," she said, and he saw something in her eyes. Something that had him wanting to reach over, touch her hair, that sleek short bob skimming to her chin. So different from when she'd been young. When touching had been easy and natural and they'd been crazy about each other.

Ethan shoved back his chair and stood. He'd seen the nameplate on the door of the interview room when he stood on the threshold of her office. The office of Meg, the cop. Meg, the woman he barely recognized.

She rose with him. Their eyes held. A long moment passed and all he could think was how nearly two decades had altered little of her physique. She retained those same long lean bones, but, tall as she was, the top of her head still remained below his chin.

He turned and walked across the hall, flicked on the light.

"Ethan," she said as he rounded the small, stark table

marred with dozens of scuffs and scratches and initials. "I'll get to the bottom of this."

"I know you will."

She leaned in the doorway, her chief's badge glinting in the ruthless lighting. She had something on her mind, he could see, something that bowed between them, eye to eye, and he remembered days long past when tension between them was as foreign as a bluebird nesting in winter.

"It's…" she began. "It's been a long time since…"

Since they'd stood within each other's proximity. Since they'd talked, actually talked.

What do you want me to say, Meggie? That I haven't forgotten what we had once? That I wish your best friend hadn't died during prom week? That, God help me, I wanted so badly to soothe your grief, heal your heart?

"How've you been?" she asked softly, and he saw the question was genuine and came from a history long past.

"Good. Real good." Same old mundane response.

Swallowing the sudden lump in his throat, he glanced at the paper in his hand, focusing on his reason for being here—because if he didn't, he'd step across the confined space and haul her into his arms. "Look, I should get this done."

She straightened from the doorjamb. "'Course. Just leave it with Sally when you're finished. And Ethan? Thanks again." With that, she walked across to her office and closed the door.

He stared at the page. In his chest, his heart hammered. Well, it was a start, this dialogue between them. The proverbial ice had been broken. So where did he take it from here?

Think about her later.

He set aside her pen, drew the ever-present pencil from his shirt pocket. Trouble was, he'd *never* stopped thinking about Meggie McKee.

* * *

In the sanctuary of her office, Meg sat at her desk, propped her elbows on its surface and put her face in her hands. *Ethan.*

Still the rescuer of wild creatures. Still healer of the hurt. A thousand memories besieged her of a teenage Ethan, holding a maimed squirrel, a fledgling robin with a crippled foot; working to save a car-struck doe.

Lord, the years. Here today, gone tomorrow, and before you knew it a chunk of life vanished.

He looked so familiar—yet not. Lines fanned around those quiet, earth-colored eyes she'd gazed into ten million times, eyes that understood pain and loss and bias, and had spoken to her heart from the moment they'd met when he was eight and she seven.

His hair was far longer than it had been at eighteen. Back then, he'd still been trying to squeeze into a world that often shunned him. Today, he was his own man and that hair was artfully cut into a shaggy, raven mane that touched the collar of his denim jacket. Her fingers tingled to dive into the thick mass, feel the silk slide against her fingers.

But she had no right to touch anymore. No right to *him.* She had made the choice two decades past.

Oh, the losses. She couldn't begin to tally them.

Dropping her hands, she looked at her closed door, heard the soft scrape of his boots as he came from the interview room and stopped outside her office.

Would he knock? Call her name?

No, he walked away. Away, as *she* had at seventeen.

Ethan.

It wasn't lost on Meg that he hadn't used her name during the interview. Undoubtedly, she had been a stranger, a woman he no longer recognized.

Well, wasn't that what she wanted when she'd returned to Sweet Creek six years ago, why she had not sought him out, rekindled their friendship, their *love?*

God, he'd been her best friend. She'd told Ethan things she never told a soul, not her best girlfriend, Farrah; not her brother, Ash. Not even her ex-husband.

A knock sounded. He'd returned, changed his mind. "Come in."

Dispatcher and receptionist Sally Dunn poked her head around the door. "Chief, you might want to see this before I scan it into the computer." She held a sheet of paper.

"What is it?"

"Ethan Red Wolf's...statement."

Meg tamped back a sigh. "You're going to tell me he didn't give one."

"Uh, well, actually he did. Just not the way you'd expect." The dispatcher set the page on the desk.

A drawing. He'd done a sketch, an intricately detailed sketch. For a second Meg closed her eyes. *Oh, Ethan. This is so you.* How on earth was she supposed to submit this to court, if the investigation reached that point?

"What should I do with it, Chief?" Sally toyed with the gold chain around her neck.

Meg picked up the page, tossed it onto the stack of files loading her In box. "Nothing, Sal. I'll deal with it." *With him.*

"He left his cell phone number. Should I call and have him come back?"

Meg shook her head. "I'll be taking a look out that way this morning. Need to get some pictures of the scene and the eagle over at the clinic." Deliberately changing topics in an effort to remove thoughts of Ethan in those long, lanky Wranglers, she asked, "Has Gilby left yet?" It was the deputy's turn to pick up the bagels from Old Joe's Bakery today.

"Five minutes ago."

"Good, let me know when he's back. I'm starving."

Sally laughed. "You're always starving. Sheesh, I wish I had your metabolism, grazing on carbs all day and never gaining an ounce."

"It's called being the mother of a teen, Sal. Takes a lot of stamina."

"I hear ya. Thank goodness those days are over in my house." Chuckling, the dispatcher headed out the door.

The instant she was alone again, Meg picked up Ethan's "statement." A time line wove over the page. Along it, he'd created more than a dozen sketches, each intricately detailed and described with notes. His spiky, slanted initials angled across the bottom right corner.

She identified her son and Randy Leland, read the time and date. She recognized Beau's obstinate attitude in his down-turned mouth. Randy looked out of the page with some reluctance, exactly as the boy appeared whenever he came to her house two miles east of Sweet Creek.

And a quarter mile from Ethan's place. Don't forget that, Meg.

No, she never forgot the fact as she watched the sun rise and set, ate and slept and argued with her son, just over a small bluff from the man she once loved so much she'd believed their souls were attached at the heart.

And when she had learned a year ago about his inheritance of the O'Conner place, about his plans to move into the house on land separated from hers by a narrow creek... God, she had walked around with a clog of fear in her throat for weeks. It was one thing to see him from a distance on her brother's ranch; it was another to be Ethan Red Wolf's direct and *only* neighbor.

Blinking, she focused on his portrayal of her son and Randy Leland. They weren't bad kids, just teenagers striving for independence. That's what she kept telling herself.

She studied the female figure, back to the viewer, sitting on the boulder where Ethan claimed to have discovered the raptor.

A small jolt darted through Meg. *It's me. He's drawn me at seventeen.*

When her hair had been long enough to touch her belt, when innocence colored the future.

Why? she wondered. Why would he include her in a present-day time line? And suddenly she understood. She, sitting on that megaton rock, offered directions to the scene of the crime.

Oh, yes, he knew she'd recognize the boulder. They'd sat there for hours as kids, and he'd kissed her a thousand times, touched her breasts while, over lake and mountain, they had observed a pair of adult eagles seek prey to feed their offspring.

More than that, on that rock, she and Ethan had dreamed of the home they'd build together, of the children they'd raise. Years of life and love wending into the future from that base point. So many plans.

Oh, Ethan. You never forgot.
Admit it, Meg, neither have you.

Simply put, she'd been bullheaded about burying
the key that locked her heart. But looking at her younger
self, remembering the emotion in his eyes back then, remembering those eyes today harboring secrets, she
wondered what he would say about *her* secret.

The scarred one under her shirt that said she'd been
cancer free for seven years.

Chapter Two

Fifteen minutes after Ethan left, two more complaints were called in, the first involving five overturned headstones at the Sweet Creek Cemetery to which Meg sent Gilby. Then Beth Ellen Woodley carped about a Ford Bronco parked on her lawn with Ulysses McLeod snoring off an all-night drunk behind the steering wheel.

By the time Meg eked out an hour of free time, it was nearly ten o'clock. "Sal, I'm going to Blue Mountain for a written statement from Ethan Red Wolf." She strode past the dispatcher to her private office for her notebook and digital camera. "Hopefully it won't take long, but if something—"

"Yeah, yeah," Sally grumbled, typing at the speed of light. "If the town floods or an earthquake happens, call your cell."

Chuckling, Meg grabbed one of the sesame bagels

Gilby had bought at Old Joe's. "You know me well, Sal."

"Don't talk with your mouth full."

"Yes, Mom." Her step lighter, Meg headed out the back door where the police SUV waited.

But by the time she had cleared the town's outskirts, sweat dotted her skin and two fingers tapped nervously against the steering wheel. She'd be talking with him again, twice in the same morning. Okay, on official business, but still. Six years, and they had barely nodded across the street or spoken ten words in one sitting.

She'd heard he renamed his grandfather's place. Instead of O'Conner's Fishing Dock, it was now Private Property. Meg smiled. Simple and to the point.

No, she thought. Nothing ever had been simple about Ethan Red Wolf. The man was as complex and intriguing as his ancestry. Even his name *Ethan* resembled the word *Earth,* a word suited for a man at one with his environment.

Turning down Lake Road—a strip of asphalt carving a path above the pine and rocky shores of the small mountain lake—Meg wondered again what Ethan had cataloged with those keen, dark eyes in those moments back at her office.

Certainly he'd noticed the stress lines between her eyes, the gauntness of her cheeks, that her hair was bobbed short and careless—all signatures of her job and current life.

In the sketch, he drew you with long, wavy hair.

Well, those days were gone. Today *he* had the longer hair.

Contemplating the comparisons, she nearly missed the turnoff leading on to his forty-acre property. Shadowed

by pines and golden quaking aspen, the single-lane dirt
trail wove a half mile down an easy incline to spill into
a delta of newly laid gravel.

He *had* been busy. Davis O'Conner's rectangular
house sported a fresh coat of terra-cotta paint that highlighted the reddish tint of aged pine needles on the ground.
Ochre window shutters and a matching door offered a
splash of vividness under the sweep of a roofed porch.

As Meg shut off the cruiser's ignition, she surveyed the
area. To the left of the house, the squat, slant-roofed
building the old man once used as an equipment and canoe
shed glimmered with fresh green siding. To the right, a
hundred-foot grassy trail fed into the trees to another green
structure. Ethan's photography and art studio?

Over the years she knew he'd forged a name for himself with his environmental photographs, sketches and
paintings. Paintings composed of swirls and shapes in
brilliant, bold colors. Two summers ago, she had pe-
rused several in a Billings art gallery, and more recently
bought calendars printed with his creations from Sweet
Creek's grocery and drugstore.

Noticing his pickup parked in front of the new green
structure, she headed in its direction—and saw what the
house blocked.

A thirty-foot weeping willow, its leaves aged gold,
stood like a sentinel beside a partially renovated wooden
pier, on which Ethan crouched, tool belt around his
hips, hammer in his hand.

As she came around the rear of the house, he rose
slowly, lifting his red cap to scrape back loose strands
of hair before settling the visor low over his eyes again.
A rottweiler she hadn't noticed climbed to its feet and
trotted down the dock.

"Lila." Ethan's low tone carried across the distance. "Be nice."

Halting, the dog watched Meg walk forward. "Aren't you the prettiest lady?" She kept her voice gentle as the wary animal sniffed her proffered fist. "Bet you're a great watchdog." Carefully, she stroked the animal's broad head and finally received a hiney wriggle of welcome.

The peace of the place curled around Meg in soft measure: the breeze towing the leaves, a chickadee's trill, Canada geese grousing their route southward—and everywhere the fundamental scent of mountain, water and earth assembling for winter.

And Ethan.

Ethan in work boots, ragged denim cutoffs and a white T-shirt, waiting motionless, a somber expression on his face.

"Ethan," she said, stepping onto the pier.

"Meggie."

For the moment she'd let the name stand. The year Doug had sent her the divorce papers she'd become Meg, a name with maturity. Only her family still called her Meggie, though her sister-in-law called her Meg. In the past two years, she and Rachel had *become* sisters; Ash's wife understood Meg's requirement for emotional strength and distance from the woman she had been once.

But Ethan lived in the past, saw her as the girl she'd been in another life. His sketch told of his memories. Memories she'd buried aeons before.

"I need to take some photographs of the spot where you found the eagle," she said. "Do you have time to come along?"

He studied her. "You know where it is."

She did; the boulder glared like a thumbprint in his diagram, and from the dock where she stood, she could see a section of beige rock across the water. "I'd like you to walk me through the scene, explain what you witnessed, a sort of reenactment." Her gaze settled on him. "I'll also need a written statement, Ethan."

For the first time, the edges of his mouth lifted and amusement sparked in his eyes. "Can't use the visual in court, huh?"

She felt a grin threaten in response. "Not when the judge knows you're well-read." He had been in high school.

He stared across the lake. "Will you catch the guy?"

The guy. Though he'd alluded to Beau in her office, his words indicated he didn't consider her son the culprit. Relief slipped down her spine. "I'll do my best."

Unhooking his tool belt, he stepped past her. "We can take my truck around to Ted's Landing, then walk in from there." Turning, he eyed her uniform shoes. "Got hiking boots with you?"

"I do." She'd learned early in her career to keep a change of clothes in her vehicle.

"Good. You'll need them."

About to say, "I grew up around here, remember?" she clamped her mouth shut. Within the tranquil ambiance, the comment seemed crass, and besides, he was heading for the shed carrying his tools, intent on her request.

Starting for her car, Meg glanced again at the house. How had she not noticed the broad cedar deck off his kitchen door? Deep planters and a trellis swaddled in leafy vines enclosed the platform, rendering it cozy and secluded. A pair of wooden Adirondack chairs painted green looked out toward the water, mountain and low hills.

What she wouldn't give to sit in one of those chairs on an evening and just let the world...vanish.

She needed a vacation. Far away. On some bleached-sand beach. With drinks in tall, dewy glasses.

Meg frowned. *Yeah, right.* Like she had time to sit dawdling away time at some commercialized resort.

With a last look at Ethan's Eden, she returned to her PC, changed her footwear, then retrieved camera and notebook from her duty bag. *Move it or lose it, Meg.*

She ignored the double entendre at the sight of Ethan heading for his truck. Was she prepared to reestablish their friendship, or would she let him go...again?

He drove with the window down, left arm on the sill, shifting the gear shift effortlessly on curves and hills. She watched his booted feet work the clutch and gas.

A small waterfall streamed through her abdomen at the sight of his bare brown calves and knees, forearms and biceps. She imagined their strength, the texture of compact muscle, how his skin—the color of dark-roast coffee with cream—would contrast against the paleness of her own.

Snapping around, she viewed the tiny lake skimming through the trees beyond the side window. What was she doing, thinking of skin and muscle and color—of Ethan Red Wolf—*this* way? She had trained herself never to think of men sexually, not for seven years, not since Doug Sutcliffe and before him...

Ethan.

Young and stupid, that's what you were back then, believing you had what it took to entice a man. Believ-

ing that, no matter what, a man would see you as a woman.

Laughable, was what it was. Laughable because here she was in what much of the world still deemed a man's job, toting a gun, wearing a mask of authority. *Hiding.*

Losing a breast to cancer tended to make a woman a tad more self-conscious. Especially when the man she'd married—the *doctor* she'd married—saw her as an altered person postsurgery.

And she would bet her badge, if Ethan knew, he wouldn't draw pictures of her with silk locks and youth on her side. He would not remember moments from an era long dead.

And he damn well wouldn't be glancing across the cab of his pickup with those eyes that embraced the secrets of the earth, and set her pulse off-kilter.

Well, to hell with him. To hell with them all. She'd gotten this far, hadn't she? Did her best to raise her son, create a secure and loving home for him, whether or not he appreciated those aspects in his hormonal, independence-seeking stage. Hadn't she?

Damn it. She just needed to stop smelling the man beside her, needed to quit inhaling the scent the sun-warmed breeze brought through the window: that musk of hard work cleaving to skin.

You're sniffing like a dog, Meg.

God, she needed a life.

Eight minutes later they arrived at Ted's Landing, a dilapidated pier so called because it had once anchored the float plane of Ted Barns—until Ted sold the plane and relocated to Kentucky.

Ethan brought the truck to a stop, dug out two iced water bottles from the glove box. After handing her one, he shoved open the door and climbed down. "We walk from here."

"I know," Meg retorted, uncapping her bottle and following him around the hood.

Did he think she couldn't recall the rugged topography around Blue Lake? And that Ted's Landing and a couple of other isolated flat acres were the only areas upon which people had built cottages and cabins? Before Ted's Landing existed, this very spot had been hers and Ethan's place to park, *their* spot to begin hiking two miles through dense bush to *their* boulder.

She stared across the miniature body of water that was more lagoon than lake. On its opposite shore, a bounty of autumn robes sheathed the rugged hills. Softening her voice, she asked, "Do you come this way often?"

He lifted a shoulder. "I circle the lake four or five times a week with my camera and sketchpad."

Almost twenty miles on foot over some of the roughest geography within the county. But then, he'd always been a man at home in the outdoors, capturing beauty others missed. In her home office, Meg had hung this year's calendar, printed with his photographs. September offered her favorite, a ladybug on a single blade of blue-eyed grass sprouting amidst a cluster of river stones.

Evidently done with talking, Ethan cut through the tumbling rock and willows edging the lake, and Meg, focusing on his back, hurried into the woods after him. Twenty minutes later, hoping the sweat under her arms lay invisible on her gray short-sleeved shirt, she followed him into blue-sky sunshine once more.

The first thing she detected was how much the place had retained its identity over the past decades, and the countless details he'd sketched in the interview room.

The elephant-sized boulder still nudged the shoreline, though cattails now led the way into the water. Behind the big stone, the cliff caught the late-morning sunshine, while willows and shaggy shrubs ascended the rock-embedded bank to the ledge that housed an immense eagles' nest. From this angle, Meg had always thought it resembled one of those behemoth ladies' hats popular in the 1920s.

"That thing must weigh a ton," she remarked, staring up eighty feet. "Do they still come back every spring?"

From under the bill of his ball cap, his eyes were mystic. "It's not the same pair, Meggie."

That had been here when they were teenagers. Kissing on that rock.

"Of course not. I was just wondering if this spring's pair returned the way the others did."

"The nest was empty for a lot of years with the shooting range so near. This spring is the first I saw a pair return to nest."

"I'm sorry, Ethan. I know how much you loved the eagles."

His eyes were fathomless under the cap's visor. "So did you."

She had. As teenagers, they'd hidden among the trees and between kisses observed the birds with telescopes and binoculars, recording hatching times and feeding times and behaviors of both parents and young.

Taking a swig of her water, Meg stepped toward the boulder. "Show me where you found the injured bird."

They went through the procedure step by step, she clicking pictures and rewriting the statement, he describing again what he'd discovered, where he had spotted her son and Randy Leland shooting at the deadwood along the shore. She snapped close-ups of the splinters in the driftwood, then of the twenty-two shells strewn among the rocks.

When it was done she presented the statement of his verbal explanation. "Mind reading it over, ensure it's correct?" She pointed below the last paragraph. "Sign at the X."

He reached over, slashed his name across the bottom of the last page.

"You're not reading it?" She had expected him to examine every nuance of what she'd written.

He pushed the notebook more securely into her hands. "I trust you, Meggie."

How could she respond to that? Trust was not something she expected from men. Ethan hadn't trusted her in the past when she'd needed him after the death of her best friend Farrah, and Doug hadn't trusted Meg's oscillating emotions after her surgery, and Mark, the man she'd dated four years ago... He had understood even less than Doug or Ethan.

"Call me Meg," she said, focusing on the present, the tangible, the *necessary,* hoping annoyance would set in so she could have an excuse to leave. "I don't go by Meggie anymore."

He tilted back his head, took a swallow of water, eyeing her all the time. As he recapped the bottle, his mouth twitched. "You'll always be Meggie to me. Meg is the cop. Meggie is the woman."

A spear of heat pricked her stomach. She turned to go. "They're one and the same. I'm not the person you knew back then, Ethan."

His biceps brushed her shoulder as he fell in step beside her. "Can't promise to remember that."

"Well, try. By the way, thanks for coming here with me." *For giving me a statement I can file.*

"I don't think your son shot the eagle."

"That remains to be seen. He's been—" She cut off the direction of thought. Ethan Red Wolf was no longer part of her life, and she had no business burdening him with her woes about a teenager dipping his toes in dark waters.

"Been what?" Ethan prompted. His stride slowed to match hers across the uneven, tricky landscape.

She paused in the cool shadows bordering the timberline. Across the water a loon bugled its lonesome call. "Let's just say Beau has a rebellious streak."

"Normal for teenagers." The flicker of fun resurfaced. "I recall us having a streak of rebelliousness when we were sixteen."

"We weren't irresponsible," she retorted. *We didn't flick cigarettes out car windows or write graffiti on the sides of buildings.* "If we had, our parents would've kicked butt."

Beneath the cap, his eyes laughed. "Oh, Meggie. You forget so easily. What about the time we did doughnut spins in my old truck across old man Freeley's hay field? And the time you drove your dad's pickup to the drive-in without permission. He sent the cops looking for us."

Her lips pursed to hide a smile. "That was different."

"How so?"

"We did it for fun. Beau's got ten miles of attitude. He does things with intent."

Ethan frowned. "You're talking like a cop, not a mother."

"Maybe I can't separate the two."

"Like you can't separate the cop from the woman?"

She walked away from him, into the forest. "This conversation's over."

"Why, because I hit a nerve?"

"Because my relationship with Beau is none of your concern."

"What about the relationship between you and me?" he called.

"A two-hour reunion isn't a relationship."

Several seconds later his fingers closed around her forearm. A pinch of fear rushed through Meg. He'd come up behind her, quick and silent, and they were on a mountainside, but most of all she had no tool of comparison for this somber-eyed Ethan to the one she'd suppressed in the memories of her past.

Scowling, he released his grip and stepped back. "Christ, Meggie. You know I'd never hurt you."

Shame warmed her cheeks. He always could read her emotions. "It's not that."

"Isn't it?"

"Look, this is my point. We no longer know each other."

"We have a history," he argued. "A long history. Which you chose to throw away by running off and marrying some other man."

"I did not run off or *throw* away anything. You chose not to *understand*."

"I understood full well. Your best friend committed suicide six days before prom night and you were so distraught all you wanted was to eradicate the memory. 'Please, Ethan,' you begged. 'Help me erase the memory. Give me something else to put in its place.' Well, sorry for not having the enthusiasm to take your virginity just so you could grab what I thought should be a sweet and tender first time for *both* of us, just to use it as a crutch in your grief. I *loved* you, Meggie. Didn't that mean anything to you?"

From a far distance in her mind, the up-and-down motion of his chest registered. He breathed as if he'd sprinted a mile uphill. Resurrected, that night still bothered him.

Suddenly, she saw herself as he had. Walking away, crying and cursing him in the same breath. Without empathy for his broken heart, his gentle soul. Farrah had been his friend, too—along with Kell Tanner. Four kids growing up together. "Buds all the way," they'd repeated on a thousand and one occasions, like a mantra.

Until Farrah made them a trio and life as they knew it died at the end of a rope in that closet with her.

As Meg stood looking up at Ethan, she remembered, too, the taunting words she'd said, words no better than those Linc Leland and Jock Ralston uttered years ago….

That night, after they'd changed from prom finery into jeans and sweatshirts, they had come here and she'd accused Ethan of letting them get to him, letting them victimize him. Like Farrah had been victimized.

Farrah's death shouldn't be the reason, he'd said. Shouldn't be the reason to make love. To which Meg had responded, *So, don't let it scare you away.*

And here she was, nineteen years later, the one scared away.

Scared of righting wrongs with Ethan. Of getting involved in a relationship. Most of all, *most of all,* scared of being a woman. A woman whose disease could return with a vengeance.

Oblivious of the turmoil in her head, Ethan stroked her cheek, a first in forever. "It's long past," he said quietly. His hand dropped. "Come on, let's head back."

She trailed him through the rugged, sun-speckled woods. And, watching the beacon of his white T-shirt amidst the shadows, she couldn't help but think how once, long ago, she would have followed him into eternity.

Meg waited until Beau came through the back door after school, threw his backpack on a kitchen chair and strode for the fridge. Dark hair gelled, jeans low on his hips—but not so you could see his underwear—he hung onto the door, one high-top sneaker resting on the toe of its mate.

"Hey, honey." She stood at the sink, grating carrots for a salad to go with the casserole she'd tossed together. "How was your day?"

He continued to stare inside the refrigerator. "Same."

Translation: boring, stupid, wish-I-didn't-have-to-go and I-hate-school.

Decision made, he hauled out a tub of yogurt, dug a spoon from the drawer, delved into the snack. Another time Meg would have reprimanded him for eating out of containers. These days she selected her battles.

The one about to occur was one of those diacritical choices.

She turned, set down the grater. He'd plunked himself on a kitchen chair. "Beau, I need to ask you something."

"Wha—?" His mouth was full of yogurt.

On the towel hanging from the hook above the sink, Meg wiped her hands, gathered her thoughts. At times her moody son could be provoked to anger by the slightest word.

"This morning someone came in and made a complaint. Which concerned you."

Flicking her way, his gray eyes, Doug's eyes, told nothing. Did he know? She felt a cool finger tap her spine.

"Who?" he asked.

"Ethan Red Wolf."

"The guy who took over Old Man O'Conner's rifle range?"

"*Mr.* O'Conner to you, Beau."

"Whatever."

Pick your battles, Meg. "Have you been on his property?"

Beau shrugged. "Maybe."

"When?"

"Can't 'member."

She didn't like the smirk as he dipped his head for another spoonful of yogurt. "Let me refresh your recollection then. Labor Day and the last weekend of July."

He slammed the container on the table hard enough to bounce a few blobs over the rim. "What am I, under investigation? If you've got something to say, Mom, then say it."

"All right." Meg shoved away from the counter and came to the table, where she sat down kitty-corner to her son. "Here's the deal. Mr. Red Wolf saw you on his land on both those days. He spoke to you during the last meeting. Both times you were carrying a twenty-two."

"So?"

"So first off, you know the rule about taking the gun without supervision." Doug had bought Beau the rifle for his last birthday, something Meg had vehemently opposed.

"Big deal."

"It is when you ignore my wishes, son. I'll be taking

the gun to the office in the morning. It won't be returned until you understand the consequences for your actions."

Irritated eyes rose. "Who needs a stupid gun, anyway?"

Indeed. "Second, you disregarded the No Trespassing signs on private property."

"I was crossing it to go up the mountain." His gaze skittered away. "Me'n Randy were target shooting."

"There's a range in Livingston for that, Beau. You could've asked me to take you."

"Yeah, well, Randy's embarrassed about his aim. Can't hit a barn wall, so I was showing him some tricks without getting razed by those dork friends of his dad's."

Linc Leland, son of the mayor. She could well imagine Linc's disappointment in his apprehensive son. What Beau saw in the boy, Meg couldn't fathom. Beau was a leader, Randy a follower.

She said, "Randy's problems don't give you the right—or authorization—to use someone's private property as a practice area. Or to shoot at eagles."

"Eagles?" His eyes widened. "Who said we were shooting at eagles? The Blackfoot guy?"

"Excuse me?"

The tips of Beau's ears pinked. "I mean, Mr. Red Wolf."

"Then say his name, Beau. Don't be disrespectful of someone's ancestry or heritage."

"All *right!* I get it already."

"Do you? Sometimes I wonder if you've learned anything I've taught you." She should stop, but suddenly she saw a teenage Ethan in high school, heard the taunts by Linc Leland and his friend Jock Ralston. *Hey, Tonto. Where's your horse?* She had hated those boys, but she'd hated the look in Ethan's eyes more. That shame and regret for who he was, who he would always be. She had loved him for a thousand reasons, but one rose above the rest: that he stood alone against the odds.

He'd never quite believed her. And in the end her foolish arrogance had proven him right.

To Beau she said, "You constantly go behind my back. You ignore the ground rules. I'm trying to make a living for us, Beau, but when you do things—"

"Okay. You don't have to rag on and on."

She inhaled slowly. "This morning Mr. Red Wolf found a wounded eagle in the area where he spoke with you and Randy."

"That doesn't mean we shot it. He's lying if he said that. Jeez, Mom, we know it's illegal to shoot eagles."

"Ethan didn't accuse you, just said he found an injured eagle where he'd last seen you two boys. He's asked that I do some investigating and get the matter resolved before—"

"And just like that you figured it was us shooting the bird." Beau shoved back his chair. "Figures. You never believe me, no matter what I say."

"That's not it at all."

"Forget it. Believe what you want, then. That's what you always do anyway." Spinning around, he stomped to the back door, flung it open and was outside before Meg could get around the table.

Damn it, she thought, watching him pace down the dirt path to where the battered old pickup she had bought him last spring waited.

Believe what you want, then. Her own words, echoing through the tunnel of her past. Words she had tossed Ethan the night of their prom. *Believe what they say, then. Don't stand up for yourself. Don't be the man I thought you were.*

What goes around, comes around, Meg. With a heavy sigh, she went back to grating the carrots.

Chapter Three

Beau squealed his wheels out of the yard. God, his mother made him so mad. Since she'd caught him smoking in his bedroom a year ago, she'd been on his case about every nitpicky thing.

No matter what he did, she never took his side, always questioned his marks on tests, saying if he studied harder he'd get better grades, or if he finished his assignments and listened in class he'd understand the material better.

She questioned where he went after school and on weekends, and for how long and why and whom he was going with. She didn't trust any of his friends.

Grinding gears, he hit the main road back to Sweet Creek. He didn't understand his mom anymore. Hell, he didn't understand himself anymore.

They used to be so close. Ever since his dad, wimp-ass Dr. Doug Sutcliffe, walked out on them when Beau was a little snot back in Sacramento. His mom hadn't told Beau the reasons behind the divorce, but he knew. Didn't take a brain surgeon to figure why the esteemed Dr. Doug left the family.

Pulse hammering, Beau slowed for the town limits. One of these days he was cutting out, leaving this backwater behind. Then he'd be free to do whatever he damned well wanted, whenever he damned well pleased. And to hell with both his parents.

Meg wanted to see the extent of the eagle's injuries and ask veterinarian Kell Tanner what he was able to determine.

After parking the police cruiser, she pushed through the front door of Sweet Creek's Animal Clinic, clinking the bell at the top of the jamb. In a short hallway beyond the reception area, Ethan stood with the vet; their heads turned upon her entry.

From under his ball cap, Ethan's dark serious eyes latched on Meg. A cold sweat swiped her skin. Had the eagle died?

"Hey, Meg," Kell said, eyes smiling. "Come to see my newest patient?"

Still alive. She breathed easier. "How's it doing, Doc?"

"There's a fifty-percent chance for survival. My bet is on the survival fifty."

"Good to hear." Her eyes wove back to Ethan, hoping to convey her relief for his sake. Rescuer that he was, the bird's wounds would weigh on his heart. Turning to Kell, she asked, "What were your conclusions on the injuries?"

He jerked his head toward the rear door. "I was just about to tell Ethan. Why don't you both come to the aviary and I'll explain."

They walked down the hall, Ethan tall and rangy beside her as they followed the doctor. Their hands brushed once. Outside, a roofed walkway linked the main structure to a small edifice. A sign reading Aviary hung above its door; inside, a birdcage contained the eagle.

Kell went to a small refrigerator, took a few bits of raw meat from plastic bag and walked to the raptor. White bandages wrapped its thigh and wings, and a plastic shield banded its neck. Yellow predator eyes watched them cautiously.

Ethan stood behind her shoulder, igniting a current of warmth between their bodies. He said, "Great job, Kell. As always."

"Thanks. Barring infection, this little gal should make it."

"Was she shot by a twenty-two?" Meg asked.

Kell pushed a piece of chicken through the wire mesh; the eagle gobbled the chunk. "I'm not an expert, but from the appearance of the exit wound in the thigh and from the minimal number of traumatized wing bones, it likely wasn't a high-powered weapon."

"And the tail feathers?" The bird had none.

"They were plucked, not molted."

Which meant a poacher or someone with a sadistic bent. "Thanks, Kell. Let me know if her condition deteriorates."

"Will do."

Meg walked out of the aviary.

"Meggie," Ethan called as he followed her outside into the breezeway.

She swung around. "Was the eagle unconscious when you found her?"

"Out cold. Probably hit her head on the rocks when she fell."

Meg studied the trees surrounding the clinic. A wind eddied autumn leaves into the air and along the ground. "It's possible they thought the bird was dead."

Ethan said nothing.

She slanted him a look. "You don't think so?"

"I didn't say anything."

"Which says more than words, Ethan. You always were quiet." And observant.

His mouth hinted at a smile. "Not around you."

Once, perhaps. Once they would've discussed every detail of their lives and feelings, shared hopes and dreams and planned their future—until she'd forced a separation between them.

Disillusioned, she turned to walk around the main building, for her truck.

"If it's any consolation," he said, walking beside her, "I've waited a long time for this day. I don't like how it's come about with the injury of wildlife, but I'm glad we're talking again."

She stopped at her vehicle. "Me, too." Without the old weight of silence, her heart felt lighter. Opening the truck's door, she got in behind the wheel. "See you later."

"Count on it." He walked back into the clinic, back to his eagle.

From her back porch, Meg peered through the starlit night toward the black stand of pine and birch mantling the knoll that rolled up and away from her three-acre property. A quarter mile, and on the other side of the rise, *he* slept in that lovely terra-cotta cabin.

Shivering inside her hoodie, she folded her arms against her middle, her senses attuned to the breeze rustling through the dying leaves, and the hint of early snow whispering down from the Absaroka Range.

Suddenly the wind sighed, *He's coming to see you.*

A flush warmed her skin and her heart hurried.

You're imagining things, she thought, yet her eyes strained to peel away the night.

A small thrill rushed up when he walked out of the trees, tall and illuminated by the stars. His feet made no sound, his arms swung easily at his side, his eyes, those beautiful dark eyes saw only her.

She stood riveted at the weathered railing, waiting. Waiting for him to mount the steps, to approach her. He wore buckskin leggings and a buckskin shirt draped his torso, and on his feet were red-and-white-beaded moccasins. A feather hung from a leather strand braided into his long, ebony hair.

Bewildered, she stared. She'd never known him to dress in the garments of his ancestry, to look as if he'd stepped out of another century. Throughout their adolescence, he had spurned his heritage; tried desperately to fit into the culture of his fair-skinned mother and grandfather.

He took the steps, stopped within reach.

As the question *Where've you been?* branded her mind, she frowned.

"Here, Meggie," he replied.

Confused, she shook her head. "Not always."

"Always. I've never left you." Then he took her face between his callused palms, leaned down and kissed her.

His lips were warm and soft and mobile. The way she remembered. Pressing herself against him, she banded her arms around his neck, stretched up onto her toes, searching, *wanting...*

His hand slipped into the open panel of the hoodie, gently kneaded her breasts.

Her perfect breasts. *Oooh, yes...!*

Sitting bolt upright, she gulped air. *Where...?*

Around her, night delineated the ceiling of her bedroom, the pictures on the walls, the metal railing at the foot of her mattress. Curtains fluttered at the open window and a chill breeze goose-bumped her arms. Dreaming, she'd been dreaming about Ethan and... and....

Oh, God.

With shaky fingers she touched the left side of her chest where the fake swell rose with each agitated breath.

Stupid woman, Meg. Did you think it had changed?

But, oh, in the dream...

She had been whole.

Right. You should've known something was weird when you saw Ethan in those clothes, and with that hair.

Throwing back the covers, she climbed out of bed. She needed to think. Outside. She would go outside, onto the porch. The best place to think. *Like in the dream.*

She shook her head. *Wake up, Meg. This is reality.*

On the nightstand the clock read 1:34 a.m. Grabbing her housecoat from the foot rail, she headed into the hallway and padded past Beau's closed door.

In the kitchen she stopped, shivered. Then turned and walked back down the hallway to her son's room. Quietly, she opened the door, peeked inside. The covers were in a jumbled heap, shadows playing hide-and-seek across pillows and walls. Something nudged her inside, to tiptoe to the bed.

The stars that had revealed Ethan in her dream now glanced through the window and disclosed Beau's bed. His empty bed.

Meg stared down at the sheets where her son should be, snoring gently with sleep. Her heart kicked.

"Beau?" The name echoed. Spinning around, she ran from the room. "Beau!"

Throughout the house she flicked lights, rushed out the front door. His old Chevy pickup sat parked beside her Silverado. Where was he?

"Beau!" Had he sleepwalked? He never sleepwalked.

Had someone entered the house, snatched her son while she lay in the throes of her dream?

The way Elizabeth Smart had been stolen...?

No! He'd gotten a ride from a friend....

Would he disobey his grounding?

He's sixteen, Meg. Obstinate, mutinous and desperate to shed the clutch of dependence.

Another thought flashed.

Dear God. Had he gone to confront Ethan over that damn eagle situation?

That had to be it, *had to be.* Meg flung back into the house, raced for her bedroom, her jeans and hoodie. Yes, she and Beau had their problems, but he'd never left the house in the middle of the night, and certainly not without her permission. He knew the scope of her worry barometer when it came to disregarding curfews and house rules.

Number one: *let Mom know.*

Except, the circumstances surrounding the wounded

eagle had pushed him to an emotional razor's edge. She knew that. Knew it as if he'd elucidated his resentment in a three-page essay.

From the minute he slammed out of the house yesterday, he'd gone into a class-A brood mood, which—more than target shooting without consent—incited her to ground him with no nights out for a week. The curfew had served to fuel his resentment. Tonight he'd hunched over his supper and grunted when she asked him a question. Afterward, he'd disappeared into his room, leaving Meg alone for the rest of the evening.

Please, she thought. *He's been so unpredictable lately. Don't let him do something rash.*

Keys and wallet in hand, she hurried out to her truck—and hoped Ethan was a light sleeper.

She killed the headlights and the ignition before climbing out of the truck. Upon the water's surface the moon painted its wafer-pale light. Twice in as many days she had driven to this place. His place. Next thing she knew, she'd be into a ritual.

The phone could have worked just as well, Meg.

About to get back in the truck and drive home, she heard his deep voice come through the dark.

"Out patrolling the neighborhood, Meggie?"

A shiver ran up her spine. *The dream, his voice sounds the way it had in the dream.* She remembered how his eyes had held her then, and in that interview room, and out by the boulder forty hours before.

Wood creaked. Focusing on its direction, she strained to see through the obscurity. Tall body limned in moonlight, Ethan stood on his front porch. The other morning she had envisioned earthen pots laden in blooms around its periphery, a patio table with an umbrella on the rear deck.

You're losing it, Meg. This isn't your home. And he's not your man. "Not patrolling," she said, more in control as she recalled her mission. "Looking for Beau."

"At this hour?"

"He's...not in bed. He'd been home all night, but when I woke up twenty minutes ago..." She pushed an uneasy hand through her hair. "His truck is parked in front of our house, so I thought maybe.... Never mind. I don't know why I figured he'd come here." She strode back to her Silverado.

"Wait." Ethan came down the deck steps, the rott-weiler trotting at his side.

Of course, Beau hadn't come here. The dog would've announced his presence and Ethan would have called her because he was a man of integrity—one who would recognize Beau's need to rebel the way Ethan had once rebelled against the school for not believing him about Linc and Jock.

He walked across the few feet to where she stood beside the truck. "Maybe a buddy picked him up."

Meg opened the vehicle's door. "Exactly. I should be on the phone calling his friends." What kind of cop was she? Had it been anyone else's kid, she would have given the same advice.

But it wasn't someone else's son. It was Beau. Her child.

That alone was reason to call Gilby, her second-in-command, get him to initiate the search. She was too close, too emotional.

With shaky fingers she tried to insert the key into the ignition.

Ethan set a hand on her shoulder, the simple touch easing her agitation. He'd always been able to soothe her fears years ago, too. Fears about her brother's dyslexia or her dad holding the ranch together. All Ethan had to do was speak her name or touch her cheek and her world settled.

"Move over," he said now. "I'll drive."

"I'm okay. I'm a cop, for heaven's sake."

He leaned in, took the keys out of her grasp. "You're also a mother. Now, scoot over and let me drive. You can give me directions and focus on what needs to be done."

Suddenly the rottweiler trotted toward the trees, low growl in her throat.

"Hold on a sec." He walked around the truck's hood. "What is it, Lila? A raccoon?"

Beneath the moon's glow, Meg saw the dog lift her snout, sort through the scents layering the night wind. Pricking her ears, the animal let out a deep-throated bay and loped into the trees.

Meg grabbed the flashlight from the glove box, and jumped out of the pickup to rush around the hood, toward the black-silhouetted woods where Ethan strode, a shadow against shadows.

"Maybe it's a coyote," she called.

An unexpected pop sounded.

Gunshot?

She stopped, heart in her throat. "Ethan?" Immediately she snapped off the flashlight and tucked the tool into the hip pocket of her jeans. "Eth?" Oh, God, where was he?

Silence.

Why had the dog quit barking?

Peering through the night, Meg whispered again, "Ethan? Answer me." *Please.*

Pop!

Ethan!

Had he been hit? *Please, no. We've just gotten together…*

Right hand automatically going to her hip where her Smith & Wesson 9 mm was belted on workdays, Meg raced for the trees. Why, *why* hadn't she brought the gun tonight? *Because you were looking for your son, not for criminals.*

"Stay back, Meggie." His voice came quietly from somewhere in the woods.

"Where are you?" she hissed, pushing branches out of her face, stumbling on a root. *"Damn it!* Ethan, get back here. Let me handle this. You don't know what you're dealing with."

Pulse beating a race pace, she halted. Thank God he was alive. But where?

The lake's wind swished against the brittle leaves. She wheeled around.

Silently Ethan peeled away from a cottonwood.

"God almighty!" She nearly clocked him with the flashlight.

"Easy," he murmured in her ear. "That thing will only serve to irritate your opponent, Meggie m'girl." Humor highlighted his words.

Disregarding the endearment, the one he'd used when they were teenagers, when he'd been crazy about her, she snapped, "Go back to your porch." Anger and worry vied for dominance in her chest. "Let me handle this."

"You're not armed."

"Doesn't matter. I'm the police and *that* gives me the experience. I'll go after Lila. You stay here."

"Like hell. It's my dog."

Stepping in front of him, she pressed her palms against his chest, and felt the wonderful warm dampness of his sweat beneath fabric and the power that hadn't been there at eighteen. "Ethan, for once don't argue. If Beau is involved it's my responsibility."

"I'm going after my dog, Meggie," he said stubbornly. "And your son. Are you with me or not?"

A lightning current flashed between them and for a moment memories of bygone years welled; she wanted to fling herself into his arms, those strong arms that waited at his sides, waiting for her.

Are you with me or not? Exactly what she had said one warm June night across the lagoon as she ranted at him about principles and being a man.

Shaking off guilt and remorse, she stepped free. "I know what I'm doing. This is my job." *And my son is missing.* "Go home. Please." She softened her voice. "If there's a problem, I'll call you on my cell. Besides, I'll need you to direct backup." In case it was required.

Turning, she plowed deeper into the forest, heading for the dog once again barking in the timber. If only she could turn on her flashlight. *Right, and be a target for the gun-happy shooter.*

If there was a gun-happy shooter.

Don't let it be Beau.

Her toe caught a raised root, pitching her forward, and a hand grasped her shoulder. Adrenaline spiked through her body, lifted the hair on her head. "Damn it, Ethan," she said, when she could speak. "Don't you ever listen?"

"All the time," he whispered against her hair, and her stomach spun at the feel of his mouth. "Be still and wait a sec, okay?"

They did. The forest lay hushed. Where was Lila? Beau? *Had* he done the shooting?

Or…had someone shot at Beau? The thought paralyzed Meg.

Shaking her head, she pushed forward. *Think like a cop, Meg. Forget everything else.*

A shout ricocheted through the night. Then came a shrill whistle—and a third shot. Somewhere within the black menacing trees, Lila went into a frenzy.

Dodging branches, Meg crested the knoll. A treeless patch gleamed under stars and moon. Beyond the narrow open space, more trees…and a glimmer of fire.

"Damn it." She dashed through the grass, but Ethan was faster, his legs longer.

"This way." He entered the trees directly above the spot where flames flickered.

Drinkers. She should have known. Images of forest fires and burning homes flitted across the screen of her mind. All at once Lila, tongue lolling, hind end wriggling, ran out of the night.

"Good girl," Ethan soothed, patting the rottweiler's sleek head. Gesturing with his hand, the dog came to heel.

They could see the campfire clearly. Meg counted six people: three girls cuddling on boys' knees. She scanned the area illuminated by the firelight. Where was the gun?

"Think the dog's gone?" Lynn Osgood asked, turning her face to eighteen-year-old Miles, son of Jock Ralston, the high school bully when Meg and Ethan attended Sweet Creek High.

"Damn right," Miles boasted. "I scared the crap out of it. It won't be back."

"Hey, we should do this every weekend."

Beau. He had his back to Meg and was snuggling Zena Phillips.

"Shoot at dogs?" Zena wanted to know.

Chuckling, he nuzzled her neck. "No, silly. I mean party hardy."

Meg wanted to throttle him. Before she could take the situation in hand, Randy Leland piped up, "Hey, Beau, how'd you get outta your grounding anyway?"

A shrug. "My mom's clueless around me."

The bluster in his voice and the girls' giggles prodded Meg forward. *That's what you think, buster.*

"Meggie, wait," Ethan whispered.

No way. She stepped into the firelight. "Hi, Beau," she said calmly. "Who's clueless now?"

The boy leaped from the log, spilling Zena to the ground. "Mom! What the hell are you doing here?"

All except Miles scrambled to their feet as Ethan stepped into the light, Lila at his side.

"Where'd *he* come from?" Randy muttered.

Meg glowered around the group. "Who brought the beer?"

"Like we're telling *you.*" Miles puffed out his youthful chest.

"And you're underage, Mr. Ralston." Her gaze caught Beau's defiant one. "All of you are, so take this is as a warning. Next time you'll be facing the juvie judge. Pack it up. Party's over."

"Next time you won't find us," Beau said, tone full of heroism for his friends. His gaze darted among them.

"Actually, *Chief,*" Miles Ralston sneered, then turned to Ethan. "Oops, got it wrong. This here's the real chief." The kid lifted a hand, palm out. "Yo—"

Meg saw red, saw Jock Ralston two decades before.

"Miles Ralston. Get off that log, get your stuff together and *leave*."

His lip curled as he rose slowly, a smart-mouthed boy in a man's body. "Try and make me."

She stepped into his space. He wasn't lanky like Beau, but fit and muscled and she had to look up into his face. "Let's get a few things straight. This is private property. Second, none of you is of legal drinking age. Third, campfires are prohibited this time of year."

"We don't give a sh—"

"*I* do," she interrupted. "And so does Mr. Red Wolf." She glanced at Ethan, hoped he could read the message in her eyes. *I'm with you.* "This is *his* land now. If you are not out of here in ten seconds, I will haul you down to the station. Got that?"

A silence fell.

The boy shrugged. "Let's blow this pop stand," he said to the others. "Too many chiefs around here."

Letting his comment go, Meg picked up the twenty-two propped against a nearby tree, checked the cartridge. "This yours, Miles?" She pocketed the chambered bullet.

"Yeah." A two-syllable word.

"Come by the office tomorrow with your dad. You'll get it back then."

Within seconds the teenagers had slipped into the night-shrouded woods. "Beau," Meg called to her son as he followed his friends.

Beside her, Ethan murmured, "Take it easy, Meggie."

The boy halted and she waited until he turned to face her. She said, "I want you in bed and asleep when I get home, understand?"

He stared at the flickering flames they had yet to douse. "You always ruin everything," he grouched.

"Not now, Beau." She did not want to fight him in front of Ethan. Tonight's situation was humiliation enough. He had seen her parenting skills—or lack of them.

But Beau wouldn't let go. "Don't you get it? You *embarrassed* me in front of my friends, playing big-shot cop."

"That's enough," Meg said.

Ethan ambled toward Beau. *No*, Meg thought. Not ambled. Moved like a cougar, all easy grace and benign power. "Don't be disrespectful to your mother."

A snort. "What, and she respects *me?*"

"Ever think she might be trying to teach you something?"

Beau looked Ethan up and down, as if the man was an insignificant blip, then her son turned and disappeared into the forest.

Meg's cheeks burned. That kind of snubbing had been part of Ethan's childhood, and now her child rubbed shoulders with a second generation of dolts.

The worst of it was Beau knew better. For sixteen years she had provided him with lessons in respect and kindness.

Now this.

She glanced over at Ethan. Moonlight swept along his broad shoulders, against a blade of cheekbone. Though the night shielded their concern, his earth-brown eyes held hers for several heartbeats.

Suddenly Meg's energy drained and she plopped onto the massive log where her son had sat not five minutes ago, hugging Zena Phillips.

"God, some days it's like he's this...this person I don't recognize." Leaning forward, elbows on knees, she stared at the licking flames of the campfire and gusted a breath. "We lock horns on everything. Friends,

school, his driving ability, meals, curfews.... Where's
that little boy I raised?"

She felt rather than heard Ethan slip onto the wood
beside her. Their arms and hips bumped as he emulated
her position. The urge to lay her head on his shoulder
overwhelmed her, and for a moment she forced herself
to keep her body still.

After a long minute he said, "He's seeking his independence, just like we did at that age."

"That may be. Doesn't mean I have to like how and
with whom he's doing the seeking."

He looked at her, a little amused. "We used to do the
same thing, Meggie."

"We never drank. Or ran around with fools."

"No...but we did a lot of this." He picked up her left
hand, bounced it gently on his big, callused palm. "And
a lot of this." Between his thumb and forefinger, he
stroked each of her paler fingers. "And this," his voice
lowered as he spread his hand, and she did the same,
matching finger on finger.

Light on dark. Delicate on strong.

Slowly he closed the gaps between his fingers so her
hand lay flat and narrow on his warm one for a few
seconds before he reopened his fingers to entwine
around Meg's. "We couldn't stop touching."

Or kissing, she thought, enthralled by his voice, the
strength of his bones and knuckles. The color of his
skin.

"We weren't so different, Meggie," he said, and she
heard gravel in his voice.

The ebbing fire burnished his cheekbones while the
heat of his touch ignited her blood. All she had to do
was turn her head, and his mouth would meet hers. She

sensed him waiting. Waiting for her next move. For her permission.

In the smoldering coals, she saw the dream again, felt the kiss he'd given, the stroke of his hands. Her body shifted toward him, toward the magnetism that was Ethan Red Wolf.

The rottweiler walked over, lay down with a grunt at Ethan's feet, and with a shudder Meg shot out of her trance.

What am I doing? She had to get home, see to her son. She had responsibilities, a life, a career. God, what had made her think she could sit here dreaming dreams she'd given up to pride a thousand years ago?

She jumped to her feet, and the crisp night air stole the sheltering warmth of his body. "I have to go," she said, kicking dirt and stones onto the dying embers of the campfire.

He rose to assist. "Sure." When night claimed the area again, when the last coal winked out, and she would have walked into the woods, he said, "Meggie, I'm glad I was here to help. If there's anything else I can do, let me know."

She stood across the deadened fire's circle of rocks. Starlight danced in his black hair, and he had held her hand for the first time in nineteen years, and she had almost kissed him. *Really* kissed him.

Looking at the dusty fire pit, she said, "Beau will make this up to you."

"That's not necessary."

"It is. This is your land. He needs to take responsibility for his actions." She lifted the twenty-two into the crook of her arm. "Do you need help around your place? Maybe with finishing the pier?"

The dog stood at his side, ready for direction from

her master, who laid a hand on her head. "If working off his consequences is what you want, then, yeah, I could put him to work."

"Fine. I'll have him there around nine tomorrow." Saturday.

She headed the way they had come, back through the trees, back to Ethan's house and her truck, back to her solitary memories, while the imprint of his hand on hers burned other memories into her skin.

And a history of regret.

Chapter Four

Ethan looked over his shoulder when Lila growled. The dog rose to her feet from where she'd been lying in a block of sunlight streaming through the studio's screen door.

"Easy, girl." He set down the photos he'd been examining on the drafting table. "That's probably our guest." Through the window he saw Beau's pickup pull up to the house.

So. The kid obeyed his mother. Before driving away last night, Meggie had been adamant Beau be accountable for his actions.

Hell, yes, Ethan could use an extra pair of hands, but having her son around for a week meant *she* would be checking up on the boy, which meant discussions and more of those long-eyed looks. That the kid was the conduit bringing her here felt like a fish bone in the throat.

Speaking softly to Lila, "Be nice," he stepped onto the stoop and into the sunshine.

"Is he gonna bite?" Beau called, hesitating inside the open door of his truck as the dog trotted toward him.

"Not unless you give her reason to."

"Terrific. She probably hates me after last night."

Ethan remained where he was. "Did you pop shots at my dog along with Miles Ralston?"

A scowl. "No-*o*."

"Then you got nothing to worry about." He gave the dog a few seconds to sniff the kid's sneakers and hands before commanding her to return. Ethan headed for the shed and his tools. Over his shoulder he said, "If you got gloves, bring 'em."

"Just so you know I think this is stupid." The truck door slammed.

Ethan didn't look back. If the kid left, that would be that. He would call Meggie, tell her to dream up another consequence plan. Without him.

"I told my mom this is slave labor."

Ethan grunted. Kid was sticking.

Inside the shed he strapped on his tool belt, collected a hammer and a sack of nails, shoved them into a box. Beau appeared in the doorway, blocking the sun for a moment before he stepped over the threshold.

"Cool," he said, wandering to the Merrimack canoe resting upside down on a pair of wooden sawhorses. "We gonna fix this?"

"Nope." Ethan set the box into the boy's hands. "We're working on the pier. These are your tools. Take care of them because they're the only extras I have. You lose them, you buy new ones."

Beau smirked. "You mean my mom'll buy them."

Ethan went out the door. "No. I mean *you'll* buy them."

"Well," the kid's tone was smug, "since I don't have a job, guess *you'll* be out of luck. No tools, no work."

Ethan stopped, lifted his cap, scraped back his damp hair. "I own a half-dozen shovels, Beau. Trust me, you won't be out of jobs to do." Lila at his heels, he continued toward the dock.

"My dad isn't going to like this, you know."

"See those nails popping up?" Ethan pointed to several rusted nail heads standing a half inch out of the wood. "Pull them out and toss them in the box. Hammer a new one in place. If the board's split or there's soft rot, pull it up and we'll replace it."

Beau dropped the box at his feet. The tools clinked. "Did you hear what I said?"

"I heard." Ethan knelt and yanked on a nail. "Your dad won't like this."

"Do you know who he is?"

He did. Doug Sutcliffe was a plastic surgeon in Sacramento. Ethan had heard the news of Meggie's marriage—and divorce—from his former employer and friend, Ash McKee, Meggie's brother. "Who he is doesn't matter, Beau. What matters is that people conduct themselves in a good and decent manner."

"You saying my dad isn't good and decent?" A thread of disquiet under the belligerence.

"I'm sure he is." *But when was the last time he saw you?*

Beau crouched at the far end of the dock, yanked nails left and right. "You got something on your mind, spit it out."

"If I had a son smart as you, I wouldn't be living in California." Ethan nodded at the hammer the boy held. "Make sure you replace the old nails. Don't just pull them."

The kid squatted. *Bang* went the hammer. "You don't know anything about my dad." *Bang-bang-bang.*

"You're right. I don't."

"Every time I go to California, he pays my flight down. We do things together." The bravado was back. The same bravado from last night when the boy mouthed off in front of his friends. "He's got this pool and a membership to this club where you can play tennis all day. His wife's really nice and so are my little half sisters. They treat me like part of the family, and we go to the beach and have lunch in restaurants with patios looking out over the ocean. Sharon, that's his wife's name, she has a gardener to look after their yard and a housekeeper. Her and the kids never have to do chores. It's cool."

Ethan measured a plank with his tape measure, sawed off two inches from a new board to fit the slot.

Beau continued, "Last night I told my mom I want to live with my dad after I graduate this year."

Ethan proceeded to hammer in the plank. "What did she say?"

"That we'll see. She thinks my dad won't want me living with him. She's wrong. My dad's always asking me to come down."

Ethan sized another plank. "When was the last time you visited him?"

Under the visor of Beau's ball cap, his eyes were shadow patches. "Four—" *whack!* "—years ago." *Whack!*

When the boy was twelve. Ethan's heart took a hard roll. Years ago, he'd gone through a similar situation, yearning for the attention of his grandfather. Trouble was, Ethan's father—a rez man who'd died young—had not been Davis O'Conner's choice for his daughter, and that had caused a rift between her and Davis. Still, whenever the old man felt guilt rise he'd call on his daughter to "bring the boy around." A token visit, a token pat on the head.

Kid, Ethan thought now, *all the hoping in the world won't do a damn bit of good.* But maybe the way he was killing those nails would help ease some of the pain.

"I'm getting a job, you know?" Beau muttered. "They want weekend help at that coffee shop called Coffee Anyone? Filled out an application yesterday."

"Your mom agree?"

"She's the one who told me about it."

Well, at least the kid wasn't going behind her back.

With a woof, Lila sprang to her feet and ran across the yard as a silver car followed the trail to the studio. Ethan frowned. Hudson Leland. Again.

"What's the mayor want?" Beau asked when the man climbed from his car and walked toward them.

"What he's been wanting for the past four months, I suspect," Ethan bent to measure another piece of wood for replacement.

"Ethan," the man greeted.

"Here to hassle me about that lease again, Mayor?" Ethan hooked his hammer onto his tool belt.

The man harrumphed. "Hassle's a pretty strong word, son."

Ethan snorted softly. *I'm not your son.* "Twice a month since April is getting a bit much, don't you think?"

Mayor Leland slipped his hands into the pockets of his khakis and jingled his change, a habit Ethan knew came from frustration. "Look, Ethan. Town council met Thursday night to discuss this…situation between us. We're willing to pay double on the lease if you'll let us get through the next three months. Only *three months*. Not a year like Jock's been wanting. Just one season, one more Mounted Shoot competition after the Harvest Moon Dayz craft fair."

Ethan got to his feet. A half head taller than the barrel-chested mayor, he saw pink scalp peeping through brown hair. He was glad the Mounted Shoot was no more. It was damned dangerous riding horses at a gallop and shooting at targets. "It's still no, Mayor. I notified council last spring. You've had nearly six months to find a new shooting range."

"Isn't that easy. People are hesitant to have guns going off near their homes. *Your granddaddy* didn't care because that hill," he gestured to the incline behind the shed, "blocked most of the sound and there was never a worry about a stray bullet."

Ethan kept his gaze steady. "I'm not my grandfather."

Leland released an irritated huff of air. "No, that's a fact. You're not. Dave was an honorable member of the community."

"That wouldn't be a slanderous statement on my account, would it Mr. Mayor?"

"'Course not. All I'm asking for is a little assistance to ease us over the hump. We're getting phone calls and e-mail complaints from all over the county since we had to cancel the Mounted Shoot. And, if you must know, folks are damned upset it won't be bringing the tourism bucks anymore."

"I'm sorry to hear that, but I don't think it's fair to hold me accountable for Sweet Creek's economy."

Ethan walked to the new planks stacked on the ground near the weeping willow. "However—" he shouldered two boards "—I'm building a therapeutic riding retreat for troubled kids on those ten acres, so you'll get a bit of your *tourism* back."

The mayor removed his sunglasses, stared at Ethan. "You're kidding, right?"

"No, sir. Already started building the paddock and stable. I plan to finish them over the next two months before the weather gets bad."

"Who do you expect to fund all that?"

Ethan dropped the planks to the dock with a clatter. "For the time being I am. But I'm also applying for grants. The retreat is something I've been thinking about for a while." Years ago, at a Texas rodeo, he'd been introduced to an instructor of such a riding academy. The woman's passion to help abused and grieving kids had connected with Ethan. All he'd thought about for months was that if kids like himself or Farrah, Meggie's best friend, had had some sort of healing outlet during their years at school, who knows how their futures would have turned out? Maybe he and Meggie would've married, and Farrah would be alive today.

Leland's eyes narrowed. "Is this venture because you worked for Tom McKee?"

A silence fell. In the distance of his brain, Ethan recognized Beau's attention. Beau, whose grandfather was Tom McKee, a man who had lost parts of both legs and left arm in the Vietnam War. "This conversation is over, Mr. Mayor."

The man's gaze whipped to Meggie's son sitting twenty feet down the dock. "Give my regards to your mother, boy." Hard eyes turned on Ethan. "Think about my offer. The money will be in your favor for that retreat." Leland walked back to his car.

"Is he right?" Beau asked, watching the mayor drive away. "Are you doing it because of my grandfather?"

Ethan pounded a nail. Initially, it had been Meggie's dream for disabled kids, but since Texas he'd wanted to include troubled kids. Like Farrah. And kids without a sense of belonging—the way he'd once felt. "It'll be for any kid who needs a friend," he said.

The boy wrenched out another rusted nail. "Cool."

Ethan concealed a smile. The day had righted itself.

Under a setting sun that left a fiery brand along the crest of Blue Mountain and gilded the leaves of the weeping willow, she observed him paddle the canoe slowly toward his dock. Dusk had edged down the mountain's timbered face, swathing long shadows into cattails and reeds, and from their hidden depths a late-migrating loon sent a quivering call.

As before, a peace and harmony settled in her bones. But more so because of Ethan, with his earth eyes and quiet stroke of paddle to water—a stroke as gentle and sure as she had seen in the pencil sketch he'd left at the station last week.

His shaggy hair lay thick and black as night against the collar of his orange life preserver. Beneath it, against the cooling evening temperature, he wore a blue flannel shirt.

With barely a splash, he pulled up beside the dock and caught hold of a post. Like a living masthead, Lila stood in the stern, her forepaws positioned on a woven nylon seat. At her master's soft command, the dog leaped from craft to pier, then trotted toward Meg.

"Hey, girl," she said, patting the canine's glossy black coat. "You're a regular lookout in that canoe."

Chortling, Ethan anchored the craft. "Since her puppy days that's been her spot. She's very possessive about it."

"I don't blame her." Meg observed him shoulder the camera pack, then bend to pick up the paddle. "It's the best spot in the boat."

His lips curved as he and Meg started for the shed. "Canoe, Meggie. There's a considerable difference."

"Like calling a ship a yacht?"

"Pretty much."

They walked side by side up the trail, arms brushing now and again. She forced herself to concentrate on the reason she had driven onto his property. "How did it go today with Beau?"

"Great. He's a quick study. And a hard worker."

Delight rushed in—for about two beats. "Don't let him fool you. He is not a fan of this situation." *Or of me.*

Her son had made that quite clear before she had sent him to pay his dues with Ethan this morning and again when the boy came home a half hour ago with blisters on his hands and a sunburn on the nape of his neck.

"I can't work there tomorrow," he'd told her the instant he stepped into the kitchen and showed her the results of the day. Her mother's heart longed to agree. Instead she'd examined the wounds carefully, handed over a tube of ointment and several bandages and told him he *would* be going back tomorrow.

He'd stormed off to his bedroom.

Fifteen minutes later, needing to thank Ethan for today and see if he was still open to working with her son for the remainder of the week, she'd picked up the kitchen phone—and overheard Beau muttering to Zena about "the whole stupid friggin' thing."

Meg had returned the receiver to its base, written a quick note, then grabbed her keys and driven the mile of winding road around the hill to Ethan's.

As they reached the shed, he glanced at her. "I wasn't so different, Meggie. Every time my mother wanted me to help around the shop, I had other plans." A crease winked in his cheek as he set the camera pack on what appeared to be a new wooden stoop. "Most of them had to do with you."

"But you weren't as confrontational."

"Wasn't I? Back then I hated the world. Or have you forgotten?" Before she could respond, he flicked on the light, stepped inside and hung the paddle near an over-turned canoe. "School, other kids, the community, my mother's strict rules. Hell, to be honest, sometimes I even hated *her,* simply because she was part of the reason I was *me.* Neither Indian nor white."

A pang registered in Meg's chest. She'd been there when the handful of idiots notorious in every school bandied about cruel nicknames whenever he wandered near their space. "Beau's problems are nothing in comparison."

His dark eyes were riveted on her. "Maybe not, but he does have issues that bother him."

"Like a mother for a cop."

He pulled off the life jacket, hooked it next to the paddle. "Like a father who doesn't give a rat's ass."

That took her back. "Beau talked about Doug?"

"He didn't disclose any secrets, so don't worry." He paused until she exited, then locked the shed and picked up the camera tote where he'd left it on the stoop.

Before she could think, she caught his forearm. The contrast of warm, soft flannel and hard, strong muscle jolted through her fingers. She dropped her hand. "I'm surprised," she said, pulse suddenly erratic because he stood inches close and she could smell his skin, "that Beau would tell you anything about Doug. It's not a topic open for discussion at home."

"Why?"

She hesitated. She did not want to discuss her own insecurities. Insecurities that destroyed her marriage, but that she'd almost conquered in the succeeding years. *Almost*—until four years ago when Mark Kramer entered the picture.

She said, "Doug has another life now. Unfortunately, Beau is simply an extremity of that, so he's not always on his father's radar screen. Long story short, Doug gets to Beau whenever he thinks of it." *Like a weed in a neglected garden.* "My son's been feeling the distance for a long time now. It's—" she ran a discouraged hand through her hair "—whatever I might I say, he still thinks it's his fault."

Remembering their last argument and Beau's adamant *He's just an ass, so who cares?* she looked toward the lagoon. Its silence fed her isolation: she was a single mother raising her child without the support of a partner and it was damn hard. "When I moved back to Sweet Creek, Doug felt it best to wean himself from Beau."

"*Wean* himself?" Ethan's sharp tone jerked her from the water's hypnotic serenity.

God, Meg. What are you doing, spewing your entire life in his face? You barely know him anymore. Except, their history had not faded no matter how much she had tried to push it from her memory.

"I've got to go; I told Beau I'd be twenty minutes and it's been forty. He'll be starving. " She moved past Ethan, eager to return to the privacy of her pickup.

"Meggie."

She didn't stop or turn. "He'll be here again at nine tomorrow."

"Have him bring gloves and sunblock. It'll go easier on him."

"Will do."

Opening the truck's door, she couldn't prevent one last look back. In that second's hesitation, she felt it again, the punch to her heart he could give with those loam-dark eyes. She climbed into the cab, turned the ignition and drove away through the encroaching nightfall, not at all at ease.

Tuesday morning, Sally poked her head into Meg's office. "Can you take a call from Helen Red Wolf?"

Ethan's mother was on the line? Nodding to Sally, she picked up her phone. "Chief McKee. How can I help you, Mrs. Red Wolf?"

"Hello, Meggie." Helen's soft voice flowed into her ear. "It's been a while, hasn't it?"

Since they had last talked. Five months ago, by Meg's calculations. When Helen stopped to buy a sack of Colombian dark roast beans at Coffee, Anyone?, the local java hangout. "Last May, I believe," she replied. "We were each buying coffee and doughnuts."

"Ah, yes. I remember. You'd gotten some of the same beans I'd bought, and we'd wondered if the weather would ever turn warm. Seemed winter was unwilling to move on, what with all the sleet."

Thirty seconds worth of words. Meg wondered why

the woman remembered. Had Ethan discussed their recent reunion with Helen? Somehow Meg didn't think so. For the most part back in high school, Ethan had tried to keep their relationship private. Not because he feared his mother's interference, but because he worried the town grapevine would ferry insinuations and innuendoes about Meg to Helen, like *Meggie McKee deserves better than your son.*

"Is there something I can help you with, Mrs. Red Wolf?" she repeated.

"Yes, sorry. I'm getting off topic. I think someone broke into my shop during the night."

Meg reached for her notebook. Jotting date and time, 10:12 a.m., she pictured the garage-turned-shop on the property on the outskirts of town where Ethan had grown up as a child, where she'd sat on the porch as a teenager and spun life's dreams with him. "Any sign of forced entry?" she asked, veering back to the moment at hand.

"One of the small panes in the back door window has been broken above the hook latch I had Ethan install years ago."

"Any items missing?"

"I've checked, but let me take another look...." Meg imagined the woman scanning the collection of Native American craft and artwork she sold. "Nothing I can see offhand. It's all as it should be."

"Anything damaged or moved around?"

"No. As I said, everything is in its place."

With a bold, black pen Meg scratched down the woman's responses, flipped to a new page. "Is there someone you've had an argument with recently, Mrs. Red Wolf? Someone who might take offense to you or your shop?"

Pause. "I've lived here all my life, know most everyone. I can't think of anyone who'd do this."

Meg didn't waver. "Do you have any enemies, maybe someone you've ticked off in the shop, someone who thought they should get a piece for a cheaper price?"

"No one." Amazement riddled the woman's voice. "I've always been fair in my prices, even allowed customers to pay through exchange if they couldn't raise the money, if I felt they were honest. I'm not a merchant out to get rich, Chief. All I need is a roof over my head, food on the table and a soft bed at night for my old bones."

"I needed to ask, ma'am."

"Ma'am." A smile drifted through the phone. "I'm not a centurion, Meggie. Helen will do fine. After all, you're not a teenager, but a responsible adult with a fine young son."

"You know Beau?" The words were out before Meg could blink.

"I do. He comes into my shop about once a month just to look. He'll sit for an hour browsing my collection of prints of people like Crow Foot and Crazy Horse and Chief Plenty Coups or talk about the various artworks and legends. I think he likes history. He's fascinated by the story of Quanah Parker."

Last of the Comanche chiefs; even Meg knew the story. She sat back, stunned. Beau liked history? *Her* Beau? Then another thought sprang forward, an insidious thought, one that poked like a tongue to a toothache. *Please. Don't let it have been him.*

And there it was. As he'd maintained time and again, she didn't trust her son.

"Mrs. Red Wolf— Helen. Would you like me to contact Ethan?"

"Does he have to know?"

"Only if you wish it."

"For now I'd rather he didn't. He tends to get a little…shall we say, overprotective at times."

"All right. I'll be there in less than fifteen minutes. Meantime, put up your Closed sign and don't let anyone in the store."

A sigh wavered through the line. "Thank you, Meggie. I'll wait for you out front."

Meg set down the receiver. First Ethan now Helen. She was reuniting with the Red Wolfs around every corner.

Chapter Five

On the northern outskirts of town, she pulled up the graveled drive of the boxy fifties house she had driven past a thousand times over the past six years. Recently a fresh coat of white had been painted on the exterior walls, and the roof had gained a new patch or two. Attached to the left side of the house was a covered port and under it sat Helen's blue Ford pickup. Beside the covered port stood a small white building with green trim and roof. What had been the garage back in the seventies had long since evolved into Helen's Haven.

Notebook and camera in hand, Meg stepped from the cruiser at the same moment Helen set her watering can among the yellow-faced pansies smiling from the periphery of the shop's bricked front steps.

"That was fast," the older woman remarked, pulling

off her gardening gloves before hanging them on the can's wooden handle.

"It's two minutes from the station." Meg went forward to shake the woman's hand. "How are you, Helen?"

"It's been a long time, Meggie."

Yes, it had. "I should've come by sooner." And not let her attempts to keep Ethan at a distance of a hundred feet interfere with her desire to visit his mother. The few times Ethan brought Meg to his home while they were in high school, Helen had treated her with respect and affection, baking chocolate chip cookies for her and Ethan to share on the back porch—between kisses. "I'm sorry it took a crime to bring me back."

"Nonsense. I'm not a peer. I didn't expect you to drop by."

Like a friend.

"Thank you for being so gracious," Meg said. *It still doesn't excuse my avoidance.*

Smiling, the older woman looked down at her sweet-cheeked pansies. Except for a fanfare of lines at her eyes and few streaks of gray, Helen's fair skin and chestnut hair seemed oblivious to age, and just for an instant Meg wanted to hug her. But she and Helen had never attained that level, even when Meg dated Ethan.

She surveyed the small shop. "Had to chase away any customers yet?"

"Just Isaac Tall Bear. Shame, too, him coming all the way down from the rez."

The Crow reservation was two and a half hours away. Meg wondered about the unfamiliar red truck she'd passed on Wren Road. From the day she donned the police uniform, she'd made it her duty to recognize nearly every vehicle owned by the nine hundred plus residents of Sweet Creek, as well as a fair number of neighboring ranch vehicles.

Squinting against the morning sun, she studied the two buildings and the carport between. "Did Mr. Tall Bear say what he wanted to buy?"

"Actually he was dropping off some moccasins and beadwork." A sheepish smile touched the woman's mouth. "I always invite him for coffee and muffins and a chat before he heads back."

"He's a regular, then?"

"Yes, he brings me material about a half-dozen times a year."

Meg nodded. "Do you usually go in the back door or the front to open up?"

"Back. I put the coffee on, then get things in order."

"Okay, I'll take a look. Can you stay here in case a customer comes along?"

"Sure, just follow the path. I didn't touch anything or sweep up the glass, just like you said."

"Thanks." Meg walked along the flagstones bordered by an array of flowers. She wasn't a gardener—who had time these days?—but could admire the friendly, color-ful array Helen planted. Some purple things, a tall clump of yellow and a variety of geraniums. Those Meg recognized from her childhood home on the Flying Bar T Ranch. Inez, her stepdad's live-in nurse, and wife after her mother's death, loved the bright splash of summer's red geraniums.

Meg wondered if Helen had chosen the flowers growing in the planters around Ethan's deck.

Damn it, stop thinking about him. For the first time in six years, a man occupied her mind 24/7. All because of one injured eagle. Ethan, Healer of the Forest, as she'd once dubbed him. Years ago. Now here she was a week into their reunion—of sorts—chatting with his mother as though two decades of virtual silence hadn't glided by. She should have sent Gilby to do the investigation.

With a sigh she focused on the shop's damage. Except for the cost of replacing the entire country-paned window, repairs to the outside would be minimal. A few shards of glass scattered the three steps, and slivers filled the tiny groove where the six-inch square of pane had rested. After taking several dozen shots and jotting three pages of notes, Meg returned to the front of the shop.

"I'll need to scout the interior," she told Helen.

The store had expanded its merchandise since Meg's last visit. Back then, only a few buckskin garments, dream catchers and a bit of art and beadwork stocked the shelves. Today, myriad Native American artifacts and crafts filled three glass counters, and various articles of clothing hung from the walls and racks.

"Was there money in the till overnight?" she asked, conscious of the scent of suede mingling with jasmine, a fragrance Meg remembered when Ethan had brought her to his mother's home.

"I take the money to the bank at four every day, then take out a two-hundred-dollar float the next morning from the ATM."

Meg checked the till situated on the counter along the right wall for signs of forced entry. There were none. "I'm going to take a look at the back door. Watch the front, okay?"

"I know. Customers."

With the wooden floorboards creaking beneath her feet, Meg walked through the store slowly, her eyes searching for destruction or something amiss. Shattered glass littered the floor directly below the knob of the rear door; she took several more photos and notes.

An easy entry, she thought. *Break a tiny pane of glass, lift the inside latch and, voilà, the shop is yours.*

But why? Why break in and take nothing? Some of the beaded jackets and leggings were worth hundreds of dollars. Before she left, she'd advise Helen to chain the more expensive items to their racks or put them behind locked glass—and get an alarm system installed.

The photo corner caught her eye. Ethan's work. As Meg approached, she recognized the curving lines, the detail, the smudge and slash of color across canvas and paper. He sold in Seattle and Billings. She hadn't considered that his mother's tiny eclectic shop would carry his work.

Why not, Meg? Because he'd succeeded beyond his simple roots?

That's exactly what she'd convinced herself to believe. Ethan's work had gained prestige in the Pacific Northwest and the Dakotas, and more recently that renown extended to California where the rich often sought Native American art; in particular, pieces created by a *real* Native American. Inwardly Meg shook her head. As if there were any other kind.

"He's very talented, my son." Helen stepped beside her.

"He always was," she replied, examining part of the now familiar willow tree, the pier leading into a misty pink dawn. The same pier he'd been working on last week when she'd stopped by to take photos of the boulder, and suddenly she imagined herself on the deck, curled under an afghan against the morning cold and snuggled in one of those green Adirondack chairs, watching him paint the scene.

Get ahold of yourself, Meg. A few chats and you act like a tenth grader drawing hearts around her boyfriend's name.

Which she had done once, a millennium ago.

"He was devastated when you left, you know." Helen's voice reeled Meg into the present. She looked at the woman whose hazel eyes were full of sorrows Meg knew nothing about.

"I didn't mean for it to happen." *I was young and stupid, and now it's too late.*

"I know you didn't." Helen looked at the pier painting. "I tried to tell him then that life sometimes has other plans for us. I think he realizes it now." She smiled. "Those beautiful photos he takes, his art… He's found peace at last."

Meg had been witness to that peace, to Ethan's acceptance of himself, of who he was and where he'd come from. Something he could teach her—if she wanted. Truth be known, she still struggled to accept the ravages her cancer had left, still let herself drown in thoughts of the used-to-bes. And those peripheral thoughts of what could happen should the cancer return….

Discouraged, she scanned the back wall. "Did you check those cupboards?" She walked toward one and opened its drawer.

"Yes, before I called the station. Again, nothing unusual."

"What about this one?" Meg rattled a small locked drawer inside a cabinet.

"That one's always locked. It's where I store extra cash in case of emergency and also some extra bracelets and earrings. Since it wasn't damaged, I figured they either didn't see it or didn't bother to try to open it."

Meg stepped back. "Do you have the key?"

"Right here." Helen walked into the rear storage and retrieved a silver key from the top ledge of the shrouded window.

The instant Meg turned the lock, the drawer popped open.

"See," Helen said. "Just some cash and—" She stared. "What on earth…?"

She reached toward the drawer, but already Meg had gathered up the small bundle of feathers bound with store string.

"I don't understand," Helen protested. "Where… how. I…I don't understand," she repeated.

"Helen, are these feathers yours?"

"No. Why would I want a bunch of feathers?" Her eyes widened. "Oh, no," she said softly. "Please tell me those aren't *eagle* feathers."

"I'm not sure," Meg admitted. "But I will be submitting them to the lab for analysis and verification."

"And if they are?"

"Then we find out who broke into a locked drawer."

Wringing her hands, Helen moved a short distance away. "Please don't tell Ethan. He's already upset about that poor hurt bird." She motioned to the bundle Meg held. "This would make him very, very angry."

She could imagine. Ethan had loved animals since he'd been old enough to chortle at a dog's wagging tail, or so his mother told her years before. From what Meg gleaned of his paintings, his love of nature and wildlife hadn't changed.

"Do you think he might know who did it?"

Helen blinked. "Why on earth would he?"

"Helen, it's not an accusation, it's about getting to the bottom of who broke into your shop and why. I need to clear every avenue, and that means asking some hard-nosed questions."

Helen rubbed a spot above her left eyebrow. "I know." She looked straight at Meg. "So I'll be hard-nosed in turn. I don't know what those feathers were doing in my store, and neither will my son. We're animal lovers, Chief McKee. Not poachers."

"Did he know about the drawer and where you kept the key?"

"Of course he did. He's the one who built the drawer."

"Did anyone else know about the key, or see where you hid it?"

Helen shook her head.

"When was the last time Ethan was in the store?"

"It wasn't him, Meggie." The woman's eyes cooled.

"When, Helen?"

"Sunday afternoon. Every other week he helps take inventory and tidy the place. We rearrange the stock. Your son came along and changed the window dressing." She inclined her head toward the store's front. "Did a nice job, don't you think?"

Meg checked her astonishment. Beau had not mentioned his adjustment in Ethan's work schedule. Nor had the man himself. *Why?*

The question tumbled through her mind as she returned to the station and worked through the day. Whether Helen agreed or not, Meg had to speak to Ethan. And Beau. *It always comes back to you, doesn't it, son?*

* * *

The men were nowhere in sight when she pulled up to Ethan's house around four that afternoon and parked beside her son's pickup, then walked around to the lakeside. Ethan's truck was gone. Had Helen forewarned him about Meg's imminent arrival, prompting him to take a trip into town to survey the damage at the shop? If so, where was Beau? This week he was to assist Ethan for two hours each day after school.

Apparently, they had finished the pier. New wood shone in elegant strips down its forty-foot length. How and when had Ethan sunk those new pylons at the far end? she wondered.

Shrugging off images of brown pectorals glistening under the September sun, she headed for the back deck. No one answered her knock on the kitchen door. Similarly, both the shed and studio were silent and locked. In the middle of the yard, she paused and again admired the changes he had constructed—and once more felt a quiet settle beneath her breastbone. As he did, she lived in the woods, but her house did not exude the same calm. Each night she came home with worry in her heart that she'd find her son smoking or drinking or puffing on a joint, or trying some worse drug. She just couldn't shake the sense of urgency.

A dozen times a day she wondered where her little boy had disappeared. Not that she wanted him to stay little, but she did wish for a return of his sweet nature, the mischief in his eyes. However, those traits had come with a certain innocence. Innocence her ex-husband had flattened with his neglect.

Was it any wonder her son spilled his guts to Ethan—

a man whose past brought an understanding her troubled son sensed?

Sighing, she headed for the cruiser. Behind the wheel, she unsnapped her cell from her belt and speed dialed Ethan's home telephone. In case of emergency, she had input the number Saturday, during Beau's first work session

As expected, the machine clicked on with Ethan's deep voice: "Thanks for calling. You know what to do after the beep."

"Hey," she said. "It's Meg. Can you please call me when you get a chance? Nothing urgent, just need to ask a question." She left her number and hung up.

Short, to the point and…emotionless. No indication her heart thumped like a rabbit's foot in her chest. She reached for the key in the ignition and caught sight of Lila, loping out of the woods, straight toward her vehicle. An instant later Ethan emerged, Beau several feet behind. Tool belts hung on both their hips, and a camera was slung around Beau's neck. One of Ethan's?

Meg climbed out of the car. Ethan, black brows pinched, strode toward her.

"I just left a message on your answering machine," she called as his long, Wrangler-clad legs demolished the distance. Beneath the bill of a red ball cap, his coffee eyes moored hers.

"Problems?" he asked, stopping within a few feet, and she stared at the triangle of sweat darkening the front of his gray T-shirt.

Meg pulled her gaze back to Beau. "Hi, son." She'd ask about the camera later.

Eyes veering away, her son offered a grunt. To Ethan he said, "I'll be in the shed, getting the shovels."

"You digging something?" she asked.

"We're busy figuring out Ethan's riding center," Beau replied in a tone that told Meg she'd interfered and wasn't welcome.

As the boy started off toward the shed, Ethan called him back. "While you're working with me," he said, "you'll treat your mom with respect."

Meg saw her son's nostrils flare. "Fine," he said, then turned back, eager to escape.

Her cell rang. "Excuse me a moment." She snapped open the phone. "Chief McKee."

"Hello, Marjorie."

Only one person used the name inscribed on her birth certificate, the name she'd hated since first grade when she came to understand the difference between cute and dull.

"Doug?" She saw Beau spin around, eyes wide.

"Where are you?" her ex asked.

"Where I always am," she retorted and squelched the urge to roll her eyes. "In Sweet Creek, Montana."

"I know *that.* I'm asking where are you in Sweet Creek? Your dispatcher said you were out on a call."

Beau stood in front of Meg. "I want to talk to Dad."

She held up a hand, spoke into the phone. "Is there something I can do for you?"

Beau pulled a face. Of course she could. She could hand over the phone.

"I'm in town," Doug went on, unaware of the silent tussle between Meg and their son. "I thought we'd get together for dinner tonight. As a family."

Stunned, she darted a look at her son, then at Ethan—who pointed a finger over his shoulder, signaling he'd be in the shed. Careful not to let her anger flash at Doug's use of *family,* she said, "What are you doing here?"

"I've been in Missoula attending a seminar."

"Since when?" Today was Tuesday.

He hesitated. "Last Wednesday."

Her fingers tightened on the phone; she turned and walked away from her son's anxious eyes. "And you just *now* thought about contacting Beau?" After a week. She wanted to grind her teeth on something hard. *Inhale, Meg. Exhale, inhale.*

"You want me to go home without seeing him?"

I want you to care about your son! It's been four years since he's seen you. Frustration winning, she snapped, "Here's Beau." Ignoring Doug's protestations, she handed over the cell phone.

"Hi, Dad."

Meg swallowed the knot in her throat at the boy's eager tone and the way he squared his shoulders as he walked off for privacy.

The shed door stood open; she headed in its direction. Inside, Ethan sat on a weathered, overturned crate checking the connection of a rusted round-mouthed shovel to its long, wooden handle. He said, "Beau must be glad."

"I suppose so." She didn't understand it, but she'd witnessed this type of love-hate relationship a dozen times in her career. Kids neglected or in foster care, still wanting to go home, back to parents who cared so little. She folded her arms under her breasts. Almost tapped her toe. "This is so like Doug to breeze into town as though it hasn't been almost forty-eight months since he's seen his son."

After rummaging through a box containing a clutter of tools, Ethan selected a metal file, clasped the shovel's blade between his knees and began honing its edge. His hands were long fingered, the tips blunt, the nails knife straight. Dirt limned the cuticle of his right thumb and a half-moon smudge lay across the dusky skin of one forearm.

Her gaze settled on the red dome of his cap, its bill funneled from countless shapings by those dark sturdy fingers. His T-shirt stretched across broad shoulders. Strong, sheltering shoulders. But, she wondered, would they be willing to bear her qualms about her cancer?

Again and again the rasp of the file drew her gaze to his hands, and those powerful thighs clad in threadbare denim—one brown knee nudging from a fist-sized hole. Because she could smell the day's work on him, she rolled her lips inward and looked out the open door. If she wasn't careful, she'd have him flat on the floor, kissing him stupid.

"What is it, Meggie?" he asked softly, the file angling along the shovel's side.

She blinked. "What?"

"You sighed." He cocked his head, eyes black under the cap. "Something's on your mind."

She looked at his mouth, curved at the corners. God, she loved his mouth.

Had loved, Meg. Past tense.

He pushed back the cap, narrowed his gaze. "You came out here looking for me. Remember?"

"I wanted to ask you about your mother's shop." Stepping to the threshold of the open door, she looked down at him, clear and visible in the light. "Are you the only one besides her who knows where she keeps the key to that drawer in the back cupboard?"

His hands went motionless. "Far as I know. Why?"

"Last night someone broke into her shop via the back door."

Eyes steady on hers, he rose. "She okay?"

"She's fine," Meg said, then explained the morning's events. "Look, she didn't want you to know about this, but I need you and Beau to show me what you handled in the store on Sunday."

"Like the eagle reenactment?"

She held his gaze. "Yes."

"Are we suspects?"

We. With that one word, he'd slung an invisible arm protectively around Beau's shoulder, something she couldn't recall Doug ever doing. Swallowing hard, she said, "Unfortunately everyone's a suspect until I eliminate them."

He set the shovel aside. "Let's do it. The sooner you clear us, the sooner you find the real offender."

Standing in the doorway, she held up a hand. "You're sure about Beau." Not a question, a statement.

"About this, yes. He likes my mother and he likes her store."

"So she said." It bothered Meg to admit her son had interests of which she hadn't been aware.

Ethan's eyes reeled her into their endless depths and for a long moment she couldn't find her voice. Softly he asked, "Do *you* think he's guilty?"

"To be honest?" Her shoulders lifted with a second sigh. "I don't know what to think about my son anymore."

Ethan jerked his chin toward the door. "He's coming to see us."

Meg stepped out of the shed with Ethan.

"I'm going to see Dad," Beau told her, handing the camera to the man beside Meg.

"Sorry, son," she said. "Something's come up, so your dad will have to wait. I need you to come with us to Mrs. Red Wolf's shop."

"*Why?* Dad's flying back tomorrow morning. I want to spend every minute I can with him." He glanced at Ethan. "I won't be able to help you dig those post holes this afternoon."

"Beau." Meg held her temper on a short rope. "You are not in a position of telling Ethan, or me, that you're taking the next two hours off. What you're doing here is a consequence of your actions last Friday. That comes first. Second—"

"All right! Fine." He looked at Ethan. "Can I please make up the time Saturday so I can see my dad today?"

"Your mom's in charge, not me."

Beau's eyes pleaded. "Please, Mom?"

Meg sighed. "Saturday is Harvest Moon Dayz. You can come Sunday if Ethan still needs you."

"Thanks." Unbuckling his tool belt, he rushed into the shed.

Meg followed him inside, reexplained the situation and her request they stop at the shop.

Beau stared at her. "You think I did it? I can't believe you'd think I'd break into a store."

"Beau, you *know* how we clear people. You've heard me explain it a thousand times. You've *grown up* with the procedure, for heaven's sake. That's *all* this is."

"Yeah, right." He pushed past her, out the door and marched to the cruiser. Like the criminal he assumed she believed him to be, he slammed into the backseat.

"Damn it." Sometimes she wanted to shake her son, shake him hard enough to rattle his teeth. Stubborn little cuss.

Ethan touched her shoulder. "Let me talk to him."

"He won't listen."

"Probably not, but let me try." He offered a whisper of a smile, one that lodged a knot in her throat. Then he strode up the path.

Two minutes later a sullen Beau slouched in the front seat of the police car—and Ethan followed Meg in his pickup back into town.

If she'd had a single doubt about her son or Ethan, she had none thirty minutes later. Both went through the store describing—as much as they could remember—what they had done the previous day. Beau, constantly checking his wristwatch and sending Meg impatient looks, whipped through his activities with, "I re-arranged the posters and changed the stuff in the window. Can I go now?" He gave the damaged rear entry a mere glance as Ethan bent down to examine the shards of glass; instead, Beau tapped his watch to capture Meg's attention. "Mom, I gotta *go*. Dad's waiting."

The anxiety her son displayed had nothing to do with the break-in, and everything to do with not meeting his father on time—which had Meg breathing easier. With cops, gut instinct equaled a sixth sense, and Meg's told her Beau was innocent.

As was Ethan.

His concern for Helen's safety, as well as the cost to fix the door's window did not stem from guilt.

"Go ahead and open the shop, Helen." Meg closed her notebook, slipped the pen into her shirt pocket. She glanced at Ethan standing tall as a pillar beside his mother. "Thanks for your help. I'll be in touch the minute something develops."

He nodded, his look holding hers a beat too long. "Appreciate it." To her son heading for the front door, he called, "Have fun with your dad, Beau."

"For sure!"

Meg's heart hurt at the eagerness in her child's voice. How she hoped this visit would meet every one of his expectations, that Doug didn't disappoint, that—for once—her ex realized this flipping in and out of Beau's life left lasting scars.

She turned to trail Beau out of the shop.

"Meggie." Ethan fell in step with her. "You need anything, I'm a call away."

"Thank you." She paused at the door, saw Helen watching them from the back of the shop. Was she worried about her son's renewed interest in his long-lost girlfriend? *Sheesh, Meg. Where do you come up with this sort of thinking?*

Ethan touched her cheek, a whisper of scarred knuckle to skin. *That's where,* she thought, almost closing her eyes.

"Thanks for helping Mom," he said softly.

"Yeah." She pushed out the door, before she grabbed his face and kissed that beautiful mouth.

Chapter Six

"What's going on, son?" Helen asked, walking through the shop toward Ethan.

He turned from the window in the door, from the sight of Meggie backing out of the driveway then heading down the street, taillights flashing as she braked for the corner. "With Meggie's investigation?"

"With you and her." Hazel eyes, replicas of Davis O'Conner's, fastened on Ethan.

"Nothing's going on." He cast a look over his shoulder at the window—as if Meggie might reappear—before realizing how it must seem to his mother, this constant seeking out the woman whose face kept him awake hours into the night. "She's investigating your break-in. Which reminds me—" he stepped past his mother "—I should board up that window on the back door."

She followed him. "You're connecting with her again. And now her son is involved. Be careful."

"Her son's working off a debt, Ma. As you know. And I'm not connecting with her and she's not connecting with me." *Liar. What were those moon-eyed looks all about? Get busy, man.*

Reaching inside the cupboard he'd built years ago for small tools and supplies, he grabbed the dustpan and brush. His mother hauled over the trash bin while Ethan swept up shards and splinters of glass.

"I see how you two look at each other," Helen said. "You've never looked at a woman the way you look at her. And don't tell me I'm imagining things. I know you've never gotten over her."

"That's bull and you know it." Yanking open the door, he stepped outside and repeated the cleaning on the rear steps. "If that were the case, I'd've done something about it years ago."

His mother stood a foot inside the door, hands on her hips. She'd always been slender, but looking at her in that doorway made him recognize the girl she might have been at twenty, teaching at a reservation school—and falling in love with his father.

"And why haven't you?" she asked quietly. "It's not like she's been unavailable. She's been divorced for—"

"I know how long she's been divorced." He threw the last of the glass into the trash bin, handed her the dustpan and brush. "Put these away, okay? I'll be back in a little while."

"Where you going?"

"Home to get a piece of plywood to hammer over this window."

"This conversation isn't over, son."

"Yeah, it is, Ma. I love you and all, but my personal life is not your concern. Hasn't been since I left home." Leaving her standing in the doorway, he walked around to the front of the shop and his truck parked on the street.

He knew her comments came from worry and a deep, abiding mother love. She'd been the supporter in his grief for a dead father, the taunts as a teenager, Farrah's suicide, Meggie's move to college. Through a string of wrecked relationships with women who could not measure up because he wouldn't allow them to fit Meggie's shoes.

Lila met him with her stub tail beating the air. For a moment he sat contemplating his home. He loved the forest, the mountain, the lake. That his grandfather bequeathed him the property still amazed Ethan. Davis O'Conner had lived here as long as he could remember, and in all that time they'd talked perhaps twenty times for a handful of minutes each. Now here he sat, thirty-seven years old, owner of forty acres of rock and timber and a piece of lagoon he'd prized during each visit to his grandfather, whenever the man felt a moment's "itch" to see his grandson.

His half-Blackfoot grandson.

Two miles—and it might as well have been across the continent. The old man hadn't believed in inter-racial marriage, hadn't wanted to acknowledge Indian blood ran in his grandson's veins. The worst was when he found out Ethan was dating Meggie. He and his grandfather had had it out then.

You think it's gonna make you more white, dating her? the old man had raged. *You'll have nothing but trouble in the end. Your kids'll go through the same crap you did. You want that?*

The words had festered for years. Until Ethan realized the old man—in his skewed way—had tried to protect both his grandson and Meggie from added heartache. It hadn't stopped Ethan from comparing every woman to the one he'd been crazy about the moment she beat him in the sheep-riding contest at the Little Britches rodeo.

Then, two weeks later, in Marlin's Grocery, he'd seen her again and, while their mothers chatted, he'd walked up to Meggie, who was examining a candle shaped like an eight with a monkey peering over its top.

"When's your birthday?" he'd asked, spellbound by her crayon-blue eyes.

"August twelfth. I'm gonna be eight. Wanna come to my party?"

She had freckles like sugar sprinkles on her nose and long black eyelashes, and he said, "We're gonna be friends."

"How do you know?"

"Because my birthday is August twelfth, too, and I'll be nine."

Her eyes rounded. *"Like twins!"*

"No," he said and tried to make his skinny body taller than hers. "Best friends forever and ever."

A smile scrunched up her cheeks. "Yep, forever."

Lila's whine jarred his reverie. *God almighty.* Here he was dredging up childish conversations from three decades ago. Scraping his hands down his face, he looked out the truck window at the dog waiting for him to climb out, her brown eyes full of concern.

Ethan opened the door. Immediately the animal leaned into his knees and he gave her a devoted scratch on her warm, silky chest. "Sorry, old girl. She's got me tied up in one helluva knot." *And I don't have a clue how to untangle the mess.*

Concentrating on the plywood and tools he'd require to repair his mother's door, he walked to the shed among the yellow-toned trees. Under a stone behind the building, he found the key to unlock the door. In the center of the floor he paused, scanned the shelves, the cupboards, while on his arms, the hair stood straight.

He glanced back at Lila. Head tilted, the dog gazed up at him with a query of, *What's the problem?*

Ethan grunted. "You'd tell me if something was off, wouldn't you, girl?"

Lila wagged her tail.

Okay, his mother's situation was making him paranoid. He'd never been paranoid. Shrugging off the sense he'd missed something, he grabbed what he needed and locked up the shed. After dumping the tool kit into the truck bed, he slammed the tailgate shut and again surveyed the shed. His eyes drifted to the studio, then to the house.

Things in the house he could replace. The studio was his life.

Ethan ran up the path. His fingers fumbled with the key before the door flew open.

Nothing out of place.

Ten minutes he wandered around the room, checking photos and artwork. Inside the tiny, windowless storage, his camera equipment remained on the shelves where he'd placed it yesterday.

He locked up, then checked the house. Again nothing out of the ordinary. Relief cooled the sweat on his skin. Once more he shut the door, flipped the lock, then walked to the truck where Lila waited.

Ethan patted her head. "Later, girl." And climbed into the cab.

Yet a chill rode with him back to town.

Dressed in tan chinos and pale-green polo shirt, Doug Sutcliffe was as tall and lithe as Ethan. But, as far as Meg was concerned, that's where the similarity ended. Tennis, racquetball and the gym kept Doug's forty-one-year-old muscles honed. *A necessity in his eyes,* Meg thought wryly—considering his profession. Doug was a cosmetic reconstructive surgeon. Disproportioned and disfigured bodies were his business, his forte. During their marriage she'd seen the results of some of his "miracles."

He'd worked one on her—sort of.

He'd talked to his colleagues, selected the best surgeon—next to himself. He'd worked through the preliminaries with her, tried to set aside her fears, walked her through the entire procedure, start to finish, the day of the operation.

Later her self-consciousness had been frozen. Beyond frozen.

Like her marriage in the succeeding months.

She hadn't been able to get beyond the difference between them. Him, the Adonis aging with a God-gifted flare; she, the Medusa whose physicality had changed irrevocably.

She went into counseling, participated in group therapy, shared horror stories with other breast cancer patients and survived the insane fear, even the image in the mirror. But she hadn't overcome the bleakness of *knowing.* Knowing it was hidden and false and fortified under a few millimeters of skin, there as a reminder the demon disease could strike anytime, anywhere again, and the whole painful process—chemotherapy, hair loss, vomiting, *pain*—would commence its cycle once more. Or worse, end her life.

Except you've been cancer free for seven years. That, she knew, meant hope, a *lot* of hope with every "free" year.

As she pulled along the sidewalk curb of the hundred-year-old Blue Mountain hotel on Cardinal Street, Beau unbuckled his seat belt and flung open the door.

"Dad," he called to the blond man standing on the veranda's wide wooden deck. Beau bounded up the steps, an eager pup to see his most favorite person in the world.

"Hey, son," Doug said. "Jeez, you've shot up like a bad weed." He laughed, but Meg saw hurt dart into her son's eyes. "Bad" was a label Beau assumed she'd invented for him. But Doug knew nothing of their struggle, of their son's rebellion. Upon Beau's last visit to California, he'd been so young. Still innocent and eager to please.

Her ex pulled his son into a hug, then beamed down at Meg. "You've done a great job, Marjorie. Our son's a fine specimen." He looked Beau up and down. "Damn fine, and handsome like his father." Again he laughed, Beau joining in.

Meg snorted softly. Any fool could see her DNA dominated their son's nut-brown hair, straight nose and slightly longer eyeteeth. Her ex had given Beau his gray eyes. Not one gene more.

The man trotted down the stairs and walked to the driver's window of her truck. "Hello, Marjorie. Gorgeous as ever, I see."

"Gorgeous is a label reserved for the eight supermodels of the world, Doug."

He chuckled. "All in the eye of the beholder, as they say."

She put the car in gear. "Let me know when Beau's ready to come home."

"Have dinner with us."

She glanced at her son. His gaze veered away. "I don't think so. Beau needs you to himself for a while."

"Oh, come on, Marjorie," he said, arching back his shoulders. "We're his parents. Let's be a family for an hour or two."

"Doug, we stopped being a family eight years ago." When a mammogram showed the knot of cancer.

His smile ebbed. "That wasn't *my* choice."

Nor mine.

Except, his comments about Jeremy Spencer's job on her reconstruction had been Doug's choice. She recalled his distinct "I could've done better," which, in her opinion, meant "You don't look that great." He hadn't meant the words to cut; rather he'd viewed her surgery with clinical eyes...and found it lacking.

Found *her* lacking.

Pushing aside the memory, Meg said, "I've always taken full responsibility for the divorce, so let's not rehash dead issues."

"We've *never* hashed it out. If we had, maybe things would have been different for us. Maybe we'd still be together and I wouldn't be paying alimony every month."

She smiled. He had remarried less than a year after she returned to Montana. Which had her wondering over the years if Sharon, his current wife, had been a side treat during his marriage to Meg. "Enjoy this time with your son." *Pay him some attention.* She looked to Beau's annoyed expression. "See you later, hon. Have fun with your dad." Pressing the accelerator, she pulled from the curb. In her rearview mirror, Doug walked up the hotel steps, then stood chatting with Beau for a few seconds before they went inside.

Driving the two blocks to the police station, she hoped Doug would treat their son to some honest father-son bonding. Give him a day he won't forget.

If nothing else, Doug owed *her* that.

An hour later she saw Ethan through the trees, a flash of red flannel shirt in the dusky distance. Slowing her truck, she pulled to the side of Lake Road and wondered why he stood motionless in the middle of nowhere. Was he taking pictures? Or did he see something not quite right, something or someone up to no good?

Meg got out of her truck, shut the door quietly and caught a glint of glass in the dying sunset. Sure enough, his camera was trained on a spot across a meadow surrounded by forest. She hopped over the narrow ditch and started through the pine trees lining the road.

Meg bit her lip to hide a grin when his head snapped around the instant she broke out of the thicket. In their youth he'd always been able to sense the slightest movement in the undergrowth.

Now, a hundred feet away, she watched him lower the camera, saw the flash of white smile.

She walked toward him steadily, gun on her hip, shoes picking up fallen leaves from the dewy grass.

"There's nothing quite as appealing as seeing a man hard at work," she said, releasing her pent-up humor with a returning smile.

His gaze took in her uniform. "Same for me. Especially when it's a sexy and successful woman."

A sexy woman. A spear of heat burrowed low in her abdomen. "You trying to sweet-talk me, Mr. Red Wolf?"

"Nope, just stating a fact. On your way home, or just scouting for criminals?"

"Heading home with dinner." She'd made a quick stop at the grocery store after leaving work. "Catch anything in your lens?"

He nodded toward a tall ponderosa pine with several deadened branches near its top. "Barred owl."

"Really?" Intrigued, Meg stepped beside him. "Show me."

Moving behind her, he reached around and lifted the foot-long zoom lens to her eyes. "Look at that second dead branch."

She attempted to focus the magnifier on the tree. And forgot the owl, forgot the heaviness of the day she'd had with Beau and Doug.

All she could focus on was Ethan. And that they stood alone in the woods, at dusk. Behind her she could feel the heat of his body, the curve of his arm around her shoulder as he tilted the camera, the touch of his fingers on hers.... Every nuance set her skin tingling.

A thousand times they had stood so as kids observing eagles in flight, deer feeding, bears fishing for trout in a riverbed—through binoculars and cameras.

He had been part of the environment forever. His heritage called to the wild and ran in his blood, though as a troubled teenager he had tried to deny the fact. Yet long ago she had loved him for that wonderful ancestry.

"I don't see it," she said, trying to hide her disappointment when he took a step away.

"Are you zeroed in on the second branch?"

"Yes." She wanted him back, lining his body with hers.

"Move the camera a hair to the right."

"Ah! There it is. Oh, Ethan, it's so fine." For a moment she concentrated on the bird. "It almost looks like a spotted owl with those white dots down its back."

"The spotted owl has spots on its chest and belly—and it's larger than this guy."

"How do you know it's a guy?"

He chuckled. "I don't. I'm assuming." Again, he moved behind her shoulder. "Take the picture, Meggie."

She turned her head, ready to hand over the Nikon, ready to say, "You should," but the nearness of his face, his lips, those solemn male lips with their hint of curve at the corners, stalled the breath in her lungs.

His eyes beguiled her. And then one edge of his mouth lifted. "You're staring, Meggie," he whispered.

It was all she needed to wake out of the trance. Lord, what was she thinking? What was she doing?

"*You* should take the picture." She moved aside, pushed the camera into his hands. "Before the light fades completely."

Without hesitation, he hoisted the lens and clicked off a dozen shots, his long dark fingers changing the zoom and angle with the efficiency of the professional he'd become. On his right forefinger a thin, white scar gleamed in the twilight.

When he lowered the camera, she took his hand, ran her thumb over the length of the stringlike welt. His skin was warm. "You never did get stitches for this. I remember."

His fingers curled around hers. "I wanted a reminder."

She looked into his face, into eyes dark as the trees

beyond. "That I was the twit who slammed your fingers in my locker door?"

He smiled. "That it was the *first* time you kissed me."

She couldn't contain her own smile. "I couldn't believe I'd done it, either. I thought I'd die right there of embarrassment. I thought for sure you'd think I was the biggest dork in school."

He stroked her cheek. "I thought you were sweet and sensitive and so damned beautiful I couldn't speak, if you recall."

She did. They'd stood there gazing at each other for what seemed like two hundred years. He had caught her by surprise right after P.E. She'd been shoving her gym bag into the locker, and he'd suddenly appeared behind her to ask if she would go to the Friday-night movie with him.

It was the first time he'd asked her out. They'd been best friends for years, but that day he'd found the nerve to take it to the next level. To make them a couple.

And all she'd worried about was the scent of her sweaty clothes wafting from the locker. So she'd slammed the door shut, not aware he grasped its top.

The cut had drawn blood.

She remembered grabbing his hand, mortified at what she'd done. *"You're hurt,"* she'd said, and with a tissue from her purse, quickly wrapped the wound to stanch the bleeding.

"It'll heal," he'd told her when she was done. And, she had bent her head, closed her eyes, set her lips against the bandage and heard him whisper, "Meggie."

One word. She'd lifted her head, felt her stomach dip to her toes and back. He was the hottest boy she'd ever laid eyes on, and she couldn't wait for him to kiss her.

Finally he'd eased his finger from her hands, rasped,

"I'll pick you up at seven," before disappearing into the crowded hallway....

"We were both pretty stunned," she said now. "I'd been waiting months for you to ask me out, you know."

"And I'd been waiting months to get up the nerve."

They shared a light laugh.

"Seems we've done that a lot over the years." She looked to the ponderosa pine and its owl. Several long seconds passed.

"We've got a lot of years to catch up," he said at last.

Her heart bumped against her throat. "What are you asking, Ethan?"

"I think you know."

"You want us to start over?"

"Would that be a crime?"

"No." She dragged a hand through her hair, suddenly nervous. "I don't know. Look, let me think about it, okay?"

He refocused on the tree and its inhabitant obscured by the encroaching night. "As long as it doesn't take another nineteen years." And then he grinned, and she knew she had to get out of there before she did something dumb like throw her arms around his neck and kiss him until dawn.

"I'll let you know." She turned to tramp back to her truck.

"Meggie."

"Yes?"

"You're still the most beautiful woman I've ever known."

"And you've known a few?" she attempted to tease, glad for the dark hiding her warm face.

"I haven't been celibate for the past nineteen years, if that's what you're asking."

"It's not."

His soft laughter tripped her heart, and had her lips tweaking.

"See you later, Ethan."

She smiled all the way home. Until she remembered his conviction that she was still beautiful.

Without seeing a thing, Beau gazed at the menu the waitress had left on the table. He'd spent two hours in his dad's room on the third floor watching a dumb movie, while his dad e-mailed and worked on his computer or talked on his cell phone.

Why the heck had his dad invited him to spend time if all he planned was for Beau to sit around in a hotel room all day?

And now the waitress was trying to flirt with his dad. Beau saw how she'd stared and smiled—as if she wanted to sit on his lap the way Zena sometimes sat on Beau's lap.

His dad was married, for crying out loud. Didn't she see his wedding ring?

Beau looked around. The place was fancy. Had fancy dark wooden tables with frilly flowers and folded cloth napkins. Beau had never eaten in the Blue Falls Restaurant and probably would never again, unless his dad returned to Sweet Creek. The great Meg couldn't afford to eat in places like this.

"Decided what you want, son?" his dad asked. "The filet looks good. So does the New York steak."

Fancy food. He skimmed the sandwich column. The waitress appeared with a tray and set a jug of ice water on the table along with the glass of whiskey his dad had ordered, and the soda Beau requested.

"I'll have a buffalo burger and fries," he said.

"A burger?" His dad laughed up at the waitress. "Kids. Treat them to a nice place and all they want is a gut bomb."

Beau flushed. "Da-*ad.*"

A wink. "It's okay, Beau. My girls order the same back home."

My girls.

Back home.

Beau's throat contracted; he looked away so his dad wouldn't see the burn in his eyes. God. He wished his dad hadn't called or come to Sweet Creek. The more Beau sat and fumed, the more he wanted to leave.

My girls back home. The words bounced around his brain. He'd never been Doug Sutcliffe's kid. He knew that now. Those trips back to California…just for show.

Tossing the menu down, he slouched back in the chair. "I'm not that hungry." Under the table, nerves jiggled his foot.

"What's got into you, son?" his dad asked after he'd ordered. "You're acting like a spoiled five-year-old. I don't put up with it from my girls and—"

"I don't care."

"Pardon?"

"I don't care what you do with *your girls.*"

A long moment passed. "Is that what this is about? Your sisters?"

Through the window, Blue Mountain stood on guard, the crest golden in the setting sun. "They're not my sisters," Beau muttered.

His dad snorted. "Your half sisters, then. My blood runs in their veins same as it does yours. Much as you might not like that, it is a fact of life."

Beau turned from the window. "No, here are the

facts. You never call me, you never write or e-mail. I never hear from you unless *I call you*. And half of those times, you aren't around. Your daughters or your wife answer the phone and tell me you're out sailing or playing tennis or golfing or…or what*ever*. And I get birthday cards with Sharon signing your name. I'm not your son, Dad. Not really." Beau blinked back tears. "Why *did* you call today, anyway?"

"I wanted to see you," his dad said quietly. "I thought you and I could do something together before I head out tomorrow for Kalispell."

"I thought you were going back to California tomorrow."

His dad swirled his whiskey. "I'm meeting a couple colleagues to go hunting for a week, maybe bag some turkeys for Thanksgiving. Might even get a bear or two."

Beau stared at his father as reality settled like a stone in his stomach. This was just a minor diversion, a quick fix to smooth over the guilt of his dad's neglect of his son. Beau pushed down the rock of hurt in his throat.

He wished he wasn't always so eager to see his dad.

He wished he'd stayed working for Ethan Red Wolf. But the truth lay right next to that rock.

Beau wanted his dad's love.

He wanted Doug Sutcliffe to care about him the way Meg cared.

Shoving back his chair, he said, "Know what? I'm not hungry at all. See ya around." He started for the big wooden doors.

"Beau, wait." His dad set down the whiskey, got to his feet. *"Beau."*

He kept walking past the hostess and through the

doors. The last thing he heard was his dad calling, "Beau, damn it. Don't do this." But he didn't follow his son outside into the fast-approaching night. Not the way Beau bet he would've done for *his girls* back in California.

Chapter Seven

Meg heaved a sigh and dropped her grocery bags on the counter. Today had been longer than most with too many dead ends on the break-and-enter at Helen's shop. The feathers had been sent to Billings for analysis to determine whether they came from an eagle, and whether they had been shed during the molting season or plucked.

The latter meant the bird was dead or injured—and someone was on an illegal hunt in the area.

As she put away tins of canned goods and set produce in the refrigerator, Meg could not ignore the single element of continuity in both bird cases. *Beau.* Who had popped shots in the vicinity of the eagles' nest, and who apparently was a regular at Helen's store.

He's not the one you should be concerned about, Meg.

Intuition did not lie, and it said her son was innocent.

His agitation at the store this afternoon had not come from guilt but rather from a nervous excitement to see his father, from not knowing what to expect with Doug.

Shutting the fridge door, she wondered what to toss together for supper. Tonight she was eating alone. Where had Doug taken their son for dinner? Were they having a good time? For her son's sake, she hoped so. God, how she hoped.

Better than anyone, she knew how Doug could exist in his own world, zero in on the current file in his head. She remembered the way he could talk to her and not focus on her, his mind back at the hospital or the clinic, considering the technique he might use to repair a scar or a tummy or a jowl. *Or a breast.*

The back door opened; Beau came in, tossed his coat on a chair.

"Hey, baby," Meg greeted, glancing at the stove clock—7:14 p.m. "Didn't expect to see you home this early."

"We ate fast." Her son hurried through the kitchen, down the hall and to his bedroom. The door closed with a click.

Meg's antennae went up. No excitement or slamming of the door? Not a good sign. She went down the hall.

"Beau? Something wrong?"

"I'm fine, Mom." His voice sounded muffled. *Forlorn.*

What happened with your dad? She raised her hand, ready to tap on the wood. Should she press him for an answer? Go in, see that he was okay? Her fingers hovered over the doorknob. No. She'd leave well enough alone. He hadn't shouted, cursed, snarled.

I'm here for you, son. If you need me.

Exhaustion returned her to the kitchen where she threw together a ham and tomato sandwich on flax bread, grabbed a soda from the fridge, then hauled the afghan off the sofa and went out onto the back porch. The rocker she'd purchased three years ago squeaked but held her, wrapped in acrylic wool and warmth, like a kind grandmother.

Meg ate slowly, savoring the stillness of the night more than the taste of food. The pungency of the surrounding forest, of dying grasses and leaves and earth, drifted on the cool air, and she wondered if Ethan sat on his porch, staring in her direction. If she chose, she could walk through the woods and be on his doorstep, in his arms, in less than ten minutes.

Because he *would* reach for her, if she gave the signal. She had seen the yearning in his dark-coffee eyes today, in the meadow down the road. And in his shed. And when he had come into the police station that first day, that reunion day.

He wanted her again.

All she had to do was lift her arms, speak two words: *hold me.*

She finished the sandwich, the soda. Truth was, Ethan Red Wolf would not hold her again in this lifetime. Meg would never allow another man—even her first love—to find her *different.* Yes, it was silly to think Ethan would be like Doug, and Mark who had wanted to marry Meg—before he'd asked if and when she had their baby would she still be able to nurse it with a single breast?

A crass comment that hadn't come out the way he wanted, but she had shown him the curb, anyway. That was four years ago. She'd dated two more men since, but couldn't bring herself to move to the next level—to try intimacy.

Leaning her head back, she closed her eyes and drifted off.

A twig snapped.

Her eyes flew open.

She'd left the porch light off. Suddenly the darkness was claustrophobic, not mellow. She strained to see beyond the dense line of trees....

Something or someone walked toward the house from their direction.

"It's just me, Meggie," Ethan's voice came to her before his shape became distinct.

Her heart rate slowed and she breathed a relieving breath as she watched him walk toward the steps. *Like the dream,* she thought. He had come out of the trees and night, the way he had in her dream. Except he wore jeans and a blue flannel shirt—and his hair was in its familiar shaggy cut. No feathers or leather beaded bands.

"Lost your way, Mr. Red Wolf?" she asked, lips curving as she stayed huddled in the cocoon of her afghan.

"Hard to lose your way when there's a beautiful woman just over the hill."

"Flattery won't get you where you're going."

"And where is that?" His voice held a touch of bemusement.

Into my heart. "Up to no good." She chuckled softly. "Would you like a cup coffee?"

He stopped a few feet away, hands tucked into the pockets of his jacket. "Caffeine and I don't mix before bed. Did Beau get home okay?"

She frowned. "He came in about an hour and a half ago. Why?"

"I met him on the road about a mile out of town. Offered to give him a ride, but he said he'd rather walk." Ethan glanced at the house.

"Beau walked home?" That she hadn't realized. She thought Doug had driven him. Damn it, something *had* gone awry. Tossing the blanket aside, she got up. "He went to his room the minute he got in. I'll find out what happened."

"Meggie, wait. Let him sort this out."

"Beau was supposed to have supper with Doug. They were to have an evening together." She blew a breath. "I knew something was wrong when he came home early."

"He'll handle it," Ethan said.

She searched his expression in the obscurity. "If something's happened to make him walk home from town, then I need to know what it is, Ethan." Turning for the door, she said, "If Doug's done something—"

She felt his hands on her shoulders and froze. He'd come up the steps without a sound, without a word, to stand behind her.

"Relax, honey. The boy's home. He's okay." His voice was a murmur above her ear.

She hesitated, torn between needing to go to Beau and remaining where she was, under Ethan's hands. She hadn't expected it to feel this natural, this normal. "Ethan." The word was a sigh.

"You're a good mother, Meggie. He'll be all right."

"Thank you." She stepped out of his reach and faced him. "As always, you're the voice of reason."

"Not always." Again he closed the space between them. Touched her cheek.

And just like that she understood what he meant. That at seventeen she had wanted to be with him and make him hers, first and forever. And he'd refused. "It was a long time ago, Ethan."

His eyes enthralled her. "I should have come after you, fought harder to fix what was wrong between us."

"It wasn't just you. I had a say in my leaving." Without goodbye.

Somewhere in the night a coyote yapped and another answered high up the mountain. "It's late," Meg said. "Let's talk about this when we're not so tired."

Before she could stop him, Ethan cupped her face in his callused hands. "I want to see you again, Meggie. Outside of your job and Beau and all the other excuses that are no doubt running through your head."

"You want us…?" Her breathing shallowed.

"To date, yeah."

He still held her face, and his right thumb stroked the corner of her mouth. He leaned closer. A warm wisp of air caressed her forehead. "I also want to kiss you."

"Ethan."

"I've watched you make a home here. I've watched you raise Beau. I've never interfered or reinserted myself into your life. But these past couple weeks…. I'd like us to have another chance—if it's not too late."

Too late. Was it? She thought of Doug and Mark and of the other two men passing through her life since The Day as she had come to think of that terrifying second the doctor confirmed the unknown. That *she* possessed the monstrous C.

Ethan drew her into his arms, bent his head and set his mouth against hers.

Oh, God. She had missed this, the feel of a man's lips.

And Ethan had such great lips. Soft and emotive, stirring up the wonder of desire, the recollection of heartache. Every memory she had of them, every tear she had shed over him years ago swelled her throat. *Ethan.* She had not forgotten him. As much as she'd convinced herself of that fact, this *moment,* this *kiss* told the truth.

He had been, and was still, part of her soul.

He lifted his head, touched his forehead to hers and whispered, "I've dreamed of this, Meggie. You don't know how often. I know you married and had a child and went on with your life. We both did. But I never forgot."

"Ethan, this is too fast. We…I need time." *Like forever.*

"We'll take it slow, honey. Slow and easy."

She stepped back, setting the night between them. "We don't know each other anymore. It's not the same. *I'm* not the same."

"You're Meggie McKee. It's all that matters. Don't walk away again."

She took another step, hid her hands under her arms. "Good night. Thank you for your concern about Beau." *It's more than his father has done tonight.* And then she did exactly what Ethan had asked her not to do. She walked away, into the house, shutting the door to darkness and dreams. And him.

Meg put her empty soda can on the counter and leaned her hands on the Formica. God, what a kiss. The man had her blood humming a sweet lyric.

She shook her head. *What are you thinking, Meg? You know this can't go further.* Lord, her emotions were on a seesaw. Yes, no, maybe. If she wasn't so confused…

But, oh, how she wanted! How she wanted Ethan Red Wolf.

She had missed him. Missed him in ways she could not fathom or reason. So what should she do?

You could try. You could see. He won't be like the others.

It's too risky.

You're too scared, is all.

The cop, afraid of her own insecurities. All the counseling in the world could not get her past those insecurities, the thought of her damaged body causing Ethan to avert his gaze just once... She could not bear it. For all her bravado, Ethan finding her deficient would have her in a puddle on the floor.

The phone rang. Leaping to grab the receiver before Beau woke, she knocked over the soda can on the counter. One hand silencing the clattering can while at the same moment jerking the phone to her ear, she wondered for a split second if Ethan had decided to call from his cell. "Hello?"

"Marjorie." *Doug.* "Is Beau there?"

"It's ten-forty-five. He's sleeping."

"Oh. He got home all right, then?"

"He's home." *Whether he's all right is another story.* "It took you long enough to call, Doug."

Silence. Then, "I had a conference call with a couple of colleagues."

"Busy man," she said, sarcasm thick.

"It's not like you think, Marjorie. He walked out on me before dinner."

"He hasn't eaten?"

"Not unless he stopped at some burger joint on the way home."

"Doug, he came home over three hours ago. You couldn't have called to see if he was okay before now?"

"I told you—"

"Yes, and I heard. I think this conversation is over. Have a safe trip back to la-la land."

"Marjorie, wait. I can explain—"

"First off, it's Meg. Second, you've explained it very well." She hung up. Sighed. What had she ever seen in Doug Sutcliffe? *You weren't thinking about his personality when you lusted after him, Meg.* No, she'd been trying to erase Ethan out of her system.

Did it work?

"Mom?"

She rotated around. Beau walked into the kitchen dressed in gray pajama bottoms and a wrinkled T-shirt. His eyes were puffy and red, and a crease streaked his youthful cheek. He'd fallen asleep crying. Her heart thumped hard. "Did the phone wake you, sweetie?"

"Was that Dad?"

"It was."

"What'd he want?"

"He asked if you were home."

Beau glanced at the stove clock. "He just called now?"

"He had a business call."

"Yeah, right." He looked out the window where night lay.

"Hungry?" she asked. "There's some leftover chicken. Want a sandwich? I can make one."

He wandered to the fridge, pulled open the door, his stance sad, his angular shoulders forlorn. She wanted to wrap him in her arms the way she'd done when he was five, ten. When he'd been accepting of her comfort, and kisses could soothe the most painful ache.

"I'll have this," he said, reaching for the last two slices of the pizza she had made a couple nights before. He poured a tall glass of milk and ambled down the hall. At his door he looked back to the kitchen. "Thanks, Mom."

"For what, hon?"

"For being here." Then he went into his bedroom and closed the door.

In her bed, she lay awake with images of Beau and Ethan spiraling through her mind. Her heart wanted to cancel her son's grounding and punishment, tell him he did not need to work for Ethan anymore. Doug had deflated the boy's enthusiasm, but she also knew she could not impinge on Ethan for her ex's disregard.

And what was she going to do about Ethan? Could she trust herself to start something with him again? Could she trust *him?* And most important, if her cancer had happened during their relationship, what would he have thought, said, *done?*

Oddly, she believed he would have stood in her corner. So why not trust him now?

Her stomach fluttered at the memory of his kiss. Not the kiss of the boy she remembered, but that of a man she realized she no longer knew. An extremely virile man. She had felt the potency of him against her stomach. He wanted her.

As always, her fingers crept up the center of her chest where seven pinprick tattoos marked her radiation. Slowly she edged to her left breast, the beaten one with its scarring. Beaten but not defeated.

What would *he* think? Could she trust him with her body?

The questions looped her mind until fatigue closed her eyes and at last she drifted into forgetfulness....

She started awake, every muscle rigid, ears straining to hear what had jerked her out of the dream. Rotating her head, she saw that she'd been asleep twenty minutes, maybe less.

There it was again—

Someone pushed against her bedroom window, trying to get inside. *Beau,* Meg thought. She had to protect Beau.

Flinging back the covers, she cat dropped onto the floor, fingers slipping instinctively along the bottom shelf of her night table, searching for the snub-nosed revolver she kept there in case of an emergency.

Relief steamed through Meg when her hand found the weapon, and its familiar shape lay in her palm.

The scraping and pushing hadn't ceased. She thought of the summer's heat expanding the window's frame, gluing her spring paint job to wood around the glass. *Thank God.* She'd fought the window on several occasions in the past months, hoping to break it loose from the four-inch lift she'd managed in June before the paint job. Instead, she'd given up and inserted an outside screen to keep insects from crawling into her bedroom. She hated bugs.

Cautiously she crept along the wall toward the window. The wooden blind hung shut, and it clinked within the frame. Whoever it was had determination on his mind. To the right of the window, Meg waited, crouching low, listening at the persistent scraping.

What the heck…?

Something was chomping and chewing within inches of where she hunkered. Long and slow, air exhaled from her mouth. She could deal with an animal. But what kind? A bear? A cougar?

Teeth ground. No, a deer, most likely. A deer feeding

off the massive hydrangea bush her mother planted thirty-five years ago when she'd lived with her two children in this tiny cottage before she fell in love with Vietnam vet Tom McKee of the Flying Bar T Ranch.

Meg slumped against the wall. How many times had she found leaves and stems snipped away on that plant each summer? Deer loved her hydrangea, the only domestic bush to survive the winter—and her gardening skills. Though, this spring she'd attempted to hook planter boxes filled with petunias and pansies and geraniums on the windowsills—and then promptly forgot to water them.

Climbing to her feet, she lifted an edge of the blind and spoke softly to the deer. "Could you leave now?"

Instant silence.

Meg waited, listening.

An owl hooted and night folded into the spot where the deer had fed. Meg hadn't heard the animal bound away, and marveled at how quick and quiet wildlife lived.

She crept back to bed, her mind animated. She thought of the wounded eagle and the possibility of a community poacher. She thought of the drinking teenagers, of Helen's break-in, of those chewed hydrangeas.

Of Doug's absentminded neglect of his son.

Ethan had treated her son with more respect than his father had. Ethan, who had kissed her tonight and touched her cheek and wanted to take her out on dates.

And when she finally slept, she dreamed of Ethan, escorting Doug Sutcliffe into a desert where dry winds blew and the sun burned life out of the soil, where her ex shouted back at Meg, *"This wasn't our marriage."*

* * *

Sorting through the police mail shortly after eight o'clock Monday morning, Meg pushed through the door of the post office, and walked into Ethan's chest.

"Easy, Meggie," he said, catching her shoulders between his hands when she lost a step. "Landing butt first on the sidewalk is no way to start the day."

She huffed a laugh. "Thanks. It'd be my luck the local newspaper snapped a photo, too. I can see the headlines, Chief Hits Dead End."

"Well, you're definitely in luck. There's not a soul for two blocks. How about a coffee?"

She looked up and down the street. With the onset of shorter days the town had become slow to rise; a lone pickup was parked at the feed and supply. "All right. Want to grab one from the java joint across the street? We could sit on the bench out front, enjoy the sunshine." And she could keep an eye on her town.

He took her arm. "It's a deal."

"Don't you want to get your mail first?"

"Later." Durango harness boots beating the pavement, he ushered her into Coffee Anyone? where the scent of Columbian roast had Meg salivating.

Minutes later, a latte in hand, she sat beside Ethan on the wooden bench outside the shop.

"Beau applied to work in there," she said, wanting him to know her son was progressing.

"He'll do well, Meggie."

She sipped her coffee. "I hope so."

"I know so. He's a hard worker."

"Thank you."

He turned his head. "For what?"

"For having faith in my son."

"He's a good kid. Just needs to sort through some things."

Like why his dad never calls or e-mails, she thought. But for the moment, she let the worry slide. Call her selfish, but she wanted to enjoy these minutes with Ethan.

A cool morning breeze blew red three-cornered leaves from the maple trees the town had planted along the sidewalk twenty-five years ago. She remembered coming to town with her mother and brother years before and seeing road crews lay new cement walkways, and landscapers dig holes for sapling trees. She recalled Helen stopping to speak to Meg's mother in front of the Rite-Aid and twelve-year-old Ethan staring at Meg with eyes of chocolate—or so her eleven-year-old mind imagined.

Now the trees were mature and she and Ethan adults and those same eyes had her stomach quivering as he leaned against the brick wall, biceps to shoulder, studying her from between black lashes.

Today he wore a denim wool-lined vest over a green flannel shirt and all she could think was blue-collar clothes had never looked so sexy.

"Did you like California?" he asked, popping her silly romanticizing bubble.

She studied the empty street. "Some of it. I liked the ocean and the wine groves in the Napa Valley. I didn't like the rushed feeling that comes with city life. What about you? I heard you went south to Texas for a while."

"Texas and Wyoming. Worked construction to pay my way through law school at Texas Tech."

Her mouth dropped. Once, when they were teens and full of dreams, they had planned to open a law office together in Billings or Bozeman and put some of their earnings into a therapeutic horse stable. "I didn't know."

He shrugged. "I never put my degree to use, so it doesn't matter. Besides—" he flashed a grin "—my art makes more money."

She didn't doubt it. His paintings, sketches and photographs hung in top galleries in two states. Once in Billings, she'd wanted to buy a particular piece, an oil of seven Black Angus calves asleep in a bed of tall, spring grass under a spangled sunrise, but the price— almost three thousand dollars—had been out of her league.

"Your art," she said now, "is stunning."

He sipped his coffee. "Pays the bills." Another studious look. "Why didn't you hang out your lawyer's shingle? Ash told me you were in the top five of your class."

"Ash should keep his mouth shut." But she was pleased her brother had forwarded the information to Ethan, given him a tidbit of her life after *that* night. "I might have been at the top, but I never finished my degree." She hesitated, unsure how she could explain, and then went with honesty. "I met Doug in my second year. By my third year, I was pregnant, so I went to work part-time so he could finish med school. Don't look at me like that. It was a conscious decision. One of us had to bring home the bacon."

"I didn't say a word."

"You didn't have to, Ethan. You think I made a stupid choice. Well, you're right. I made a lot of stupid choices, starting with prom."

His hand covered hers. "Meggie, stop. Your choices weren't any worse or better than mine. I could've done more to right the problem between us. I could've encouraged us to sit down and talk it out. Instead, I chose to have a pity party and said to hell with it—with you. For that I'll never forgive myself."

A lull ensued.

Her gaze moved to his lips, to his arrow-straight raven hair—that honorable flag of his father's Blackfoot ancestry. Impulsively, she pushed her fingers up his nape and caught a fistful. He'd always had hair a girl would kill for, dense and glossy and strong. His Adam's apple shifted and a volt shot down her belly, but she didn't release the locks. Instead, her fingers came to know their texture, the contrast of softness and coarse silk.

"Your hair is amazing." Slowly, reluctantly, she withdrew her hand, her fingertips skimming a cord against his nape. "What's this?" She tugged and saw it was a leather necktie of sorts.

"A medicine pouch," he said, pulling a tanned buckskin case out from under his shirt.

Meg took the soft, three-inch square between her fingers. The artwork was exquisite. Black beads bordered the case, while its minuscule flap presented a yellow background edged by two blue bands. Between those bands stood a red wolf.

"Got it from my uncle after you left," Ethan said. "I figured if I was going to be the man you wanted, I had to embrace my heritage and stop trying to be someone I wasn't. Got a little sweetgrass inside. Supposed to help set the soul free, get rid of negativity." A quick half smile. "I'd say it worked. I stopped blaming the world. And now you're here."

"Oh, Ethan." She felt her mouth tremble. He'd accomplished what she, in the past seven years, had been unable to do for herself and still couldn't—accept self.

A hint of a smile. "You gonna cry on me, Meggie-girl?"

She sniffed, ran a wrist across her nose. "'Course not. I don't cry." *Not anymore.*

"That the tough cop speaking?" he chided.

"No, that's your Meggie speaking," she stated, realizing she'd inadvertently shown him her heart with "your Meggie." Well, she wasn't his Meggie; she was no one's Meggie. She was who she was because of her choices, good or bad. And that was Meg.

But the dispute sat like an unmanageable knot in her stomach.

Beside her Ethan tucked away the pouch and murmured softly, "Company's coming."

That Jock Ralston's initials were J.R. was no pun. The man strutting down the sidewalk toward them emulated the arrogance of J. R. Ewing from the old TV series *Dallas.*

"Well, now." The man produced a horse-toothed grin. "Isn't this cozy? Our town chief having coffee with the rural chief. Guess my boy Miles was right. You two are back at it again. How long's it been? Twenty years?"

Meg smiled pleasantly. "Your boy Miles is wrong, Councilman. But just to ease your curiosity, I'm conducting an informal interview here."

A snicker. "Now I've heard of everything. Even I know police interviews are handled at the station."

"Really? When *your* truck hit the telephone pole outside of town two summers ago, I interviewed you on the roadside, Jock."

He shifted his feet. "That was different."

"How so? Because you were driving under the influence and could barely walk?"

His pale blue eyes flicked to Ethan. "You're divulging confidential information, Chief."

"Considering the accident *and the charge* were written up in the *Rocky Times*, I'm not relaying anything the entire town doesn't already know." It still amazed her the populace had elected him to their council last fall.

As if reading her last thought, Ralston blustered, "I'll be voting you out next term."

Ethan set his hands on his thighs, straightened his spine. "Maybe the town will vote *you* out next term, Councilman."

"That a threat, Tonto?"

Meg stood up. "Enough."

Ralston barked a laugh. "Got her fighting your battles again, Red Wolf?"

Fuming, Meg bit back a retort.

Ethan rose slowly. A head taller than his childhood tormentor, he said, "I fight my own battles, Ralston. Anytime you want proof, let me know. And while we're at it we can clear the air about you losing your managerial position when I closed the rifle range."

"I don't give a rat's ass about the rifle range."

"That a fact? Then why do you keep sending the mayor out to beg me to reopen?"

"Hudson's agenda isn't mine."

"Funny. Your name keeps popping up with his every visit. Maybe you should talk to him about that. Or come out yourself and *we'll* talk."

"Wouldn't waste my time," the man sneered before pulling open the coffee shop door and stalking inside.

Meg shoved a hand through her hair. "I'm sorry. Some people simply never grow up."

"Ah, hell. Everyone knows the man has a single-digit IQ."

She looked up, her gaze direct. "Promise to stay away from him, Ethan."

"If he crosses my land—"

"Promise."

He touched her cheek, a ritual she was coming to crave. "I enjoyed having my morning coffee in the sunshine with you, Meggie." Then he walked across the street to disappear inside the post office.

She gathered her mail off the bench. The day waited at the station. Yet, as the hours ticked by, Ethan's subtle rejection of her request concerning Jock Ralston worried like a vexing mosquito.

Chapter Eight

Three minutes after five on Friday, Meg shoved a pair of files for review into her briefcase, preparing to go home. Sally had gone at four, Gilby at four-thirty.

The phone rang. "Police department."

"What're you planning for supper?" Ethan's deep voice flowed through her every fiber. She hadn't seen him all week and suddenly she knew. She'd missed him. Very much.

"I was thinking of picking up a couple burgers for Beau and me at Papa D's." Papa D's served the best hamburgers and veggie pizzas within a fifty-mile radius, and after another exhausting week, cooking was the last chore Meg wanted to begin at home. It was Friday, leftover night.

"Forget Papa D's. Come over to my place. Bring Beau. I'll throw some steaks on the grill, we'll have a little wine, watch the stars come out."

What a divine image. Around a smile, she pointed out, "Beau is planning to go to a movie tonight."

"What time?"

"They usually go to the late show."

A beat of silence. Was he thinking the same thoughts? That Beau's absence would provide an opportunity for them to be alone? *Late at night?*

"He'll still need to eat. Besides I want to thank him for his help around here. Haven't gotten around to that yet."

"All right, I'll see what I can do. Anything you'd like me to bring?"

"Nope. Just be here at six-thirty. And, Meggie? Once Beau leaves, we'll have our first date."

Dial tone. He'd hung up.

Meg lowered the receiver. *Our first date.* A trill of heat ran up her thighs. He had been thinking about the two of them alone, in his house, at night. Without a neighbor for two miles.

She pulled on her police jacket, grabbed up her briefcase and purse. In the Silverado, both hands clenching the steering wheel, she followed the headlights out of town and down Lake Road to her house.

An hour and a half, and she'd be seeing him again. An hour and a half to get ready, put makeup on, fix her hair. Find something to wear that would...

What, Meg? Catch his eye? Make him see you as a woman?

Nerves jumping, she went into the house. Beau was on his bed, texting on his cell phone.

"Hey, honey," she said, leaning in the doorway. "Feel like steak tonight? Ethan's invited us over for a feast of Montana beef."

"Nah. Me'n some friends wanna grab a pizza. Can I have some money?"

He had yet to look at Meg. "I'll leave thirty on the table."

His head snapped up. "Thirty? C'mon, Mom. It's Friday night. Can't I have fifty?"

"Thirty, Beau. Ten for your share of the pizza, twenty for the movie, popcorn and a snack afterward." He and his friends usually went for a soda or ice cream following the movie.

"What if we wanna do something else?"

"Such as?"

"I dunno. What if I need to get gas?"

"You filled up two days ago."

Flipping closed the cell phone—the one she paid the bills for—he swung off the bed to dig in his closet. "God, you're so paranoid. It's not like I'm going to get drunk, you know."

No, actually I don't. Feeling a twinge of guilt because excitement leaped in her stomach at the thought of Ethan, she said, "Would it make a difference if I extended your curfew until twelve-thirty tonight?"

He lifted a shoulder. "I guess."

Meg walked into the room where the scent of her child permeated the clothing scattered on bed, chair and desk. On impulse she kissed his youthful neck. Since the incident with his father, the tension between them had eased somewhat.

"I love you, son. Have a fun night."

"You, too," he groused, yanking a navy hoodie from a hanger. "Tell Ethan hi for me."

"I will." She turned to leave—and noticed the camera half-hidden by an abandoned jacket on his desk. Walking over to pick up the digital Nikon, she asked, "Where did you get this?"

Beau canted a look over his shoulder. "It's an old one of Ethan's."

Surprise snagged her. "Why would he give you a camera?"

He zipped the hoodie halfway. "We were talking about his photography business one day and it sounded sort of cool and I asked how he took the pictures—you know, the ones for cards and stuff?—so he showed me. I think being a photographer might be…I dunno…like a cool career, y'know?"

Meg gazed at her half-grown boy. *Ethan,* she thought. *You've done more in one week for my child than his father has in sixteen years.* For a moment she couldn't speak.

"It's no big deal, Mom."

"Oh, honey. It's a huge deal." Her eyes stung.

He hiked an indifferent shoulder. "You, um…want to see some shots I took?"

"Absolutely."

Immediately he tugged a folder from under the blotter on his cluttered desk.

"You had them developed?" she asked.

"There were a lot of poor ones, but Ethan said that's normal. He takes tons of shots and ninety percent are junk. Or so he says," Beau added, cheeks pink with abashment. "We printed these in his studio."

We. Swallowing a knot, Meg imagined Ethan guiding her son through the art of selection, the steps of printing. She stared down at the first photo, an aspen branch with each individual leaf pure gold against a cerulean sky. Next was a five-point buck almost camouflaged by its environment and ready to step from the photograph. "Beau, these are stunning."

"They're okay."

There were six in all. She saw what Ethan had recognized: her son had an eye for the most insignificant detail. Could her heart swell any further? "I'd like to frame some of these."

Beau took back the folder, shoved it into a drawer. "Like I said, it's no big deal."

But it was. She saw it in the flush on his cheeks, that mixture of embarrassment and pride. She wouldn't push. "We'll talk more later," she promised and headed for the door.

"Mom?"

"Yes?"

"I think he kinda likes you. Ethan, I mean."

"You think so?" She bit her tongue, squelching the urge to grin.

Beau dug a pair of jeans from the clean stack she had put on his dresser two days ago. "It's pretty obvious the way he looks at you. You could do worse, you know."

I have. Twice. "I'll keep that in mind." She hurried to her bedroom before she burst out crying. Or laughing. *Oh, Ethan...what am I going to do about you?*

He was waiting for her on the dark porch as she stepped from the Silverado. Muted light spilled from one window, not enough to give her access to his features, his expression, and suddenly she felt foolish for having chosen to wear a dress. A dress, for God's sake, when she hadn't worn one in six years, not since she'd become chief of police. *Not since you've been hung up about self-images.*

But tonight she'd selected the dress purchased on a whim in Billings several years ago. Back then, she had been taken by the blue hue and the way the fabric fitted her body, tucked in at her waist, swirled around her knees. She'd liked the soft, easy sense of it upon her skin and against her damaged chest.

Tonight in the mirror she recognized a woman. A woman whose eyes seemed a little haunted, a little tired, whose cheeks were more hollow than normal, but a woman who appeared unexpectedly *female*.

With a creak of wood he emerged from the obscurity to come down the porch steps. "Hey." His deep voice soothed like a sip of warm chocolate.

"Beau wasn't able to join us," she blurted, clutching her purse to her chest. "He's going with friends to Papa D's."

Halting a foot away, Ethan stroked her hair. "Don't worry so much, Meggie. We'll be okay."

She understood. She would be okay *alone* with him. Grateful for the darkness hiding the warmth stealing up her neck, she admitted, "I haven't done this in a while." A long while.

"Well then, we'll fumble along, see how it goes." The humor in his tone calmed her further. "Come inside before you get chilled." Taking her elbow, he guided her up the steps and inside the ochre-painted door.

The first thing she thought was that his stern-faced grandfather, Davis O'Conner, could not have visualized the earthy beauty of the house. This was Ethan through and through—the great room, the hardwood floors, the island buffering kitchen from living quarters.

"Your house is gorgeous," she said, eyeing the stone fireplace with its pair of navy loveseats, cozy on a Native American rug. She pictured herself curled there on long winter evenings with a mug of chocolate steaming on the table of weathered wood.

She blinked away the image.

"I'm glad you like it." He took her jacket, stopped, stared. "Wow." The word expelled on a soft breath. "You always were a beautiful woman. But tonight…" His gaze slowly brushed her body. "Forget the house. *You*…are gorgeous."

Her nerves dissolved. "You don't look half-bad yourself." *Indeed*. He'd donned a pair of black Wranglers, and a rust and tan shirt that, in the lamplight, reflected the hue of his high-boned cheeks.

And, *oh-oh-oh,* that thick hair. If she didn't tangle her fingers in its shining mass soon, she'd go crazy.

Catching her admiration, he leaned in, whispering against her ear. "Let's see if the steaks have marinated enough." Then turned to lead her, tongue-tied, into the kitchen.

Thumping her stub tail, Lila lay on the mat at the glassed patio door. Meg crouched down to stroke the animal's chin. "Hey, girl. Aren't you such a well-behaved doggie, staying here and waiting."

Ethan laughed. "She wasn't always. Busted a few things around the house with her puppy antics."

"I still have that problem at home with a kid who owns two left feet most days."

"Yeah, but the great thing is they do grow out of it— eventually. Come, sit." He pointed to a stool at the island.

Antsy, Meg said, "Let me make a salad…or whatever."

"Help yourself. Bowl's in there." He opened a low cupboard. "Ingredients are in the fridge."

A minute later he took the steaks out to the deck to

grill, and she tossed together a fresh, nutritious salad of baby spinach, almonds and late-season strawberries. She placed the bowl on a two-seater table he had set with green cloth napkins and silverware. Through the huge window facing the deck and lagoon, the night hung iridescent in stars and moonlight.

Ethan brought in several foil-wrapped potatoes. At the stove, he concocted a mixture of cut peppers, onions and mushrooms in a pan, set it to simmer while he poured her a glass of chardonnay and snapped open a soda for himself.

"You're not drinking?" Meg asked.

"Nope. Haven't in almost fifteen years."

She checked her surprise. As a teenager, he hadn't been averse to sharing a beer or two. "Why the abstinence?"

Returning to the stove, he proceeded to stir the vegetables. Had she offended him? Finally he set down the wooden spoon and turned, truth in his eyes. "I'm an alcoholic, Meggie."

Her lips parted. "I don't... This..." She couldn't find the words to finish what she wanted to say. She couldn't stop her pulse from beating slow and hard, from the questions *How? Why?* bounding around in her mind in a whirlwind of surprise.

"Door's open if you'd rather not eat at my table, Chief."

In the next heartbeat, anger planted itself. Pushing aside the salad bowl, Meg walked toward him, tilted her head and glared into those deep-earth eyes.

"I'll pretend I didn't hear that, Ethan Red Wolf. What happened to us in the last two decades has no bearing on this moment."

"Except it does." He cupped the nape of her neck,

stroked his thumb beneath her ear, easing her ire. "I wouldn't be the man I am today and you wouldn't be the woman you are. We're bringing baggage to the table, honey, and some of it may not be nice. Hell, some of it may be downright unpleasant."

Her eyes hung on his. He spoke as if he could read her soul, as if he had etched his name where her left breast once existed.

Deflated, she stepped from his warmth. "Are the steaks done?"

For an instant he said nothing, then nodded. "They are."

She dished up two plates with salad and released the foil around the potatoes; he brought in the steaks, spooned the pan mixture over the savory meat.

And somewhere between the words *alcoholic* and *steaks* they had lost footing on their camaraderie. Meg wanted it back.

He lit a squat, multicolored candle centered on a wrought-iron oak leaf between their plates, then pulled out her chair.

"The meal looks wonderful. So does your home." *So do you.* And it was true, though it wasn't the home or appearances as much as the peace, the calming effect his presence brought.

"Thanks." He took a bite of her salad, chewed, looked across the table. "Mmm, delicious." Then, "I'm sorry, Meggie."

"For what?"

"For dumping my personal junk on you when we've barely begun again."

She rose and retrieved a bottle of water she'd noticed earlier in the fridge. "The wine is lovely, but I like your choice better." Back in her chair, she raised the bottle, smiled. "To a perfect meal and perfect company."

He joined her toast. "Which includes enchanting police chiefs."

Meg slanted him a look. "Just don't break the law."

"Wouldn't dream of it."

The lines beside his eyes creased and she wanted to lean over the table, put her mouth on his. She wanted to ask him how his alcoholism had happened, how he'd allowed liquor to become the focus of his life. She wanted to erase the pain he must have endured, the cause. She wanted to touch his hair, trace the shape of his lips, touch the vee of skin in the collar of his shirt. She wanted *so much* of Ethan Red Wolf.

She picked up her fork. The stereo system filled the room with a fusion of country and easy-listening refrains. "I like your choice of music."

He cut into his steak. "Aren't you going to ask me why I became an alcoholic?"

The candle sparked its light in the window glass, his hair, his eyes.

"That was then, this is now. What we've done in the past can't be undone. Which makes rehashing it futile." *Good advice for whenever you look in the mirror, Meg.* Their eyes held, and a hot shiver broke over her flesh. The man had her wishing she were the spontaneous type. She had been once. Once, she would've got up, gone around the table and climbed into his lap.

He said, "The reason was my own insecurity. You were right, you know. I wasn't the man you would've wanted."

"Ethan, this isn't necessary—"

His hand slid across the table, covered her fingers.

"It is if we're going to do it right this time. I had a part in the way things happened between us. At eighteen, all my energy was on the chip on my shoulder that a dozer couldn't remove. Except for you. You made the world a lighter place, but even you couldn't change the dishonor in my heart." He drew back, offered a partial smile. "Lots to regret, lots to make up for."

Oh, yes, Meg knew all about regret. She carried a truckload, starting with those infamous prom-night words.

And then there was her marriage to Doug. Not that she was sorry to have married him. No, she regretted that in the end he hadn't been enough for her, that they hadn't been able to make it as a family. Doug wasn't a bad guy, just self-absorbed.

But it was the silly fears, her lack of self-confidence around Ethan she regretted above all. Because when it came right down to it, the issue lay with *her,* not with a man. Well, she was working on that with her counselor in Billings. Sort of. *Three sessions a year isn't cutting it, Meg.*

But tonight, regrets and her past had no place to roost. Instead she wanted to spend the hours looking at Ethan. She wanted to laugh with him, listen to his voice, walk in his soul.

She wanted him to kiss her.

They finished the meal and when he went out to scrape the grill clean, she gathered their plates to wash in the sink.

She was there, hands in suds, when he came back inside, stepped behind her and wrapped his arms around her middle, directly below her breasts.

He murmured her name, just her name, and she closed her eyes, drifted on sensation, on the feel of his shape—all hard angles and muscle—against her.

"You smell so good," he whispered. "Feel so good."

His lips nuzzled her hair, kissed her ear, neck, shoulder. "I never thought I'd get to do this again with you. Never thought I'd hold you again."

She was lost in his voice, his words. Her head fell back to rest against his shoulder, and his mouth trailed the line of her chin.

"When's Beau's curfew?"

"Twelve-thirty." Her mind voided when he gently nipped the skin under her jaw.

"I want to make love with you, Meggie. I want to touch you, have you touch me. I want to be inside you."

Her eyes fluttered open and she stared at the dark window glass above the sink, at their reflections. Ethan, kissing her and kissing her. She, with sultry eyes, wanton lips, sexy breasts.

A woman she did not recognize.

"Meggie," he whispered, cupping her jaw, turning her to his mouth, his fingers molding her left breast.

Vision crashed into reality and she whipped around, her soapy hands striking his chest, wetting his shirt, pushing back. "Stop, Ethan. Stop right now. I can't do this." She moved out of his embrace, hurried across the kitchen and nearly ran to the front door.

"Megs?" Stunned, he watched as she hurried to the coat closet, hauled out her jacket and tugged it on.

"The meal was lovely, Ethan. Everything was lovely, but there are things you don't…know."

Her words spurred him into action. He went to her. "Tell me."

"I can't." Not yet. Tears thickened her throat. "Look, it's late. I need to go. Again, thank you."

"Meggie." He caught her hand. "Don't go. Whatever it is, we can sort it out. If it's me—"

"It's not you. It's me. Please…"

A sigh escaped. "All right. We'll table it for the moment." He kissed her between the eyes. "I'm here if you need me."

Too much. I need you too much. "See you."

"'Night, honey." He held the door as she practically ran through it to her truck. He was still standing backlit with the golden glow of interior lamps when she drove down his lane, into the night.

Helen sat on a canvas lawn chair in the shade of the tent Ethan had set up at dawn in preparation for Saturday's Harvest Moon Dayz. For the past three hours dozens of people had wandered the seven rows of tents housing the wares of artistic community members while she worked a needle with beaded thread through the flap of a moccasin.

She'd participated in Sweet Creek's craft fair and flea market for more than twenty years, and each autumn her tent was last on the row nearest the trees.

She didn't mind. Truth be known, she preferred the spot. People tended to linger longer at her booth because it *was* the final display. She suspected after enjoying stalls with woodwork, ceramics, soaps and candles, paper crafts, handmade clothes, bonsai plants, glass and metal ornaments, as well as an array of baked goods, they had no desire to rush back to the drudgery of their day.

Across the grassy path stood Sally Dunn's shelter presenting multiple pound cakes and pies that, to Helen, were second to none. Sally, she suspected, baked her goods two days before the fair for freshness. Helen liked the police dispatcher; they had shared these same spots on the grounds behind the courthouse for too many years to count, and each Christmas she and Sally traded their goods: mince pies and Christmas cake for Blackfoot jewelry.

Today, however, Sally seemed less friendly. Oh, she'd offered the customary, "Hi, Helen. Nice day for the fair" greeting, but she hadn't uttered a word since. Neither had Helen's sales been that profitable; she'd sold five items since the fair opened at nine o'clock.

She wondered if news about the lab's statement, which Meggie had stopped to inform Helen about at the shop, had circulated around town. And whether the dispatcher had anything to do with the knowledge the feathers had been plucked, not molted.

Well, Helen couldn't worry about what other people thought. If Sally Dunn and the rest of the community believed Helen guilty or her son equally blameworthy, there was nothing further to be said.

"Want me to take over while you get some lunch and stretch your legs, Mom?" Ethan's question raised her head.

He stood tall and lean in front of her chair, succinctly blocking Sally from view.

Helen set aside the partially completed moccasin. "I could use a bite and some exercise, thanks, son."

He surveyed the three tables he had formed into the shape of a U. "Not going so well this year I see," he stated quietly as a potential customer turned and went back up the row without stopping.

With her hands against her lower back, she stretched. "It'll all blow over soon. The minute Meggie gets the person or persons responsible. Then things will be back to normal."

He snorted softly. "And if she doesn't?"

"She's a good cop, Ethan. She'll get the job done."

"Yeah, and in the meantime you suffer."

"And you worry too much. We've lived on far less in the past, as you know." She patted his arm, moved around the tables. "See you shortly."

"Take your time."

She struck off down the rows toward the periphery of the grounds. A deli sandwich from Old Joe's Bakery along with a bottle of water was the perfect solution to her growling stomach.

About to leave the fair behind the courthouse, she heard her name called. Turning, she saw Hudson Leland wend his way through the crowd. At the sight of the man, Helen's appetite vanished.

"Helen," he said, approaching. "Can I have a word with you?"

A word. There was an innovative idea. Hudson Leland hadn't said *a word* to her in almost three decades. Not since she had left his bed in shame and humiliation.

"Mr. Mayor." Her gaze darted around; she did not want to be seen talking to Hudson Leland. Her face heated. Next, Hawthorne's scarlet *A* would materialize on her forehead.

"Where are you going?" Leland asked. He hadn't chided her about the Mr. Mayor greeting, hadn't said, "It's just Hudson." No, he'd been all about power back then, and he was all about power today.

"Old Joe's." *Not that it's your business.* She started down the graveled path along the side of the courthouse, her feet picking up speed.

He fell into step. "Can I buy you coffee?"

"Why?" *We haven't spoken in thirty years and now you want to chat for thirty minutes?*

"Does there have to be a reason to buy a beautiful lady a friendly coffee, Helen?"

She faced him. "Stop right there, Mr. Mayor. First off, my days of beauty are over. Second, we've never been friends, and third, if this has something to do with my son and that rifle range his grandfather owned, I'll be standing in Ethan's corner. Just so we're straight."

His eyes narrowed, big chest puffing as he angled back his shoulders. "Oh, we're straight, don't you worry your pretty little head." Then he chuckled when her mouth tightened. "Always were a spirited little filly, weren't you, Helen?"

She turned and almost broke into a run.

"I heard you had a break-in last week," he said, his legs keeping an easy pace with her.

"It's old news."

"When it concerns my citizenry, it's never old news. And since the *Rocky Times* hasn't printed a sentence about your shop as far as news goes, this is just between you, me and the police. And the bad guy, of course." Another half laugh.

Helen said nothing. She knew part of Meg's job was to fill in the mayor about crime around town. He was, after all, her boss. But it irked Helen, nonetheless, that he'd be privy to her situation, to this part of her life.

She stopped before crossing the street to Old Joe's. "What did you want to talk about, Mayor?"

This time he tsked. "Such formality between old...friends."

The rat. He'd paused as if to say "lovers," then purposely changed his mind. And once, ages ago—*merciful heaven*—this man had held her sorrowful heart in his hands....

She'd been a part-time bookkeeper for Leland's real estate business when Jackson Red Wolf, at the age of thirty, crashed into a telephone pole during an electrical storm five miles from home. Comatose, he'd lain in the hospital for five months—and Helen had gone nearly crazy with worry trying to keep her life together and her distressed eight-year-old from failing third grade. In those months Hudson Leland offered compassion, soothing words, sympathy—which led her into utter *stupidity*. The day before Jackson died of a brain embolism, she had crawled into Leland's bed.

She'd never forgiven herself.

Yes, it happened only once. Yes, she'd told him the next day she could no longer work for him or in his business.

But the *act* had cast a shadow onto her life. A shadow that, after three decades, she still feared her son would one day detect.

She clutched her purse to her side. "As I said, we were never friends—or anything else," she pointed out, her eyes direct. *Get the message, Mr. Mayor?* "Now, if you'll excuse me, I need to buy my son some lunch."

"You can't deny what happened between us, Helen."

Halting midstride, she spoke softly, "I don't deny it because unfortunately it did happen." *Utter stupidity.* "To this day I abhor my weakness at the time." She paused. "However, I am not that same weak person today." She headed for the crosswalk.

"Does Ethan know?"

The words were quiet, a muttering under his breath. She spun around.

He smiled and it wasn't kind. "Here's the deal, *Mrs. Red Wolf*. You get your boy to change his mind about the rifle range and I'll keep our little…indiscretion, shall we say?…between us." He tipped his head, a gentleman of old. "Enjoy our Harvest Moon Dayz."

Chapter Nine

Dressed in uniform, Meg walked along the stalls, speaking to each community resident and making herself known to unfamiliar faces from out of town. Harvest Moon Dayz attracted contributors from throughout the county, in particular those selling flea market items. To Meg, a flea market was a polite way of saying "humongous garage sale," or in some cases, "outdoor pawn shop." However, she kept those thoughts to herself. The craft day had been Hudson Leland's brainchild when he served as a town councilman in the late eighties.

Still, over the years, she and her second-in-command Gilby Pierce had salvaged several stolen commodities during Harvest Moon Dayz. Two had been power tools on which the owner had carved a distinctive scratch; another was a bicycle, the fourth a lawn mower. The latter item contained the owner's last name in a covert location.

Today she paused beside a booth offering fishing tackle. The customer bartering with the merchant over a "nearly new" rod was not a local. Except for the straw cowboy hat with the three eagle feathers in its band, he looked like a businessman in pressed black chinos, polo shirt and buffed Rockports.

He zipped Meg a head to shoe glance, lingering a beat longer on her chest. Reading her nametag? Or inspecting her private commodities?

Jackass.

His gaze lifted. "Sheriff."

He'd recognized the insignia on her police shirt. She would forgive his British demeanor and accent. "Actually, it's police chief."

A smile produced a dimple. "All the better."

"Why's that, sir?" Her peripheral vision caught Ethan in a royal blue shirt two stalls down, watching them.

After digging a ten and a five from an inch-thick wad, Mr. Britain laid the bills on the table, picked up the purchased rod. "Chief has more clout." Again the dimple flashed. "And more...how do you Americans say it? Pizzazz."

"Are you from around here?" she asked, curious that he'd consider bargain stock when he could afford quality.

The dimple remained. "Am I a person of interest?"

"Are you?" she returned.

His well-shaved cheeks reddened slightly. "Unless you *need* to know, Chief, I'm at no obligation to state where I'm from. I'm simply here to acquire fishing gear."

This time she smiled. "I wasn't aware there was a law against friendly conversation." Throwing him a humorless smile, she meandered down the row. She'd keep an eye on Mr. Brit.

"What was that about?" Ethan asked when she stopped at Helen's table. His eyes were trained on the strawhat man, who offered them a salute, then disappeared into the crowd.

"Probably nothing."

"Probably?"

She shrugged. "I like to keep all avenues open."

"Should I feel safer having a cop for a girlfriend?" His grin shot straight through her heart.

"Two kisses doesn't make us a couple," she said, though her lips bowed in return.

He leaned forward. "If we didn't have an audience, I'd prove you're telling a fib, Chief Meggie."

Such beautiful eyes. She wanted to cloak their dark mystery around her. Hide within their shelter. And in that instant she knew. She would never look—*had never looked*—at another man in this way. With Ethan, she felt—

"Rory? Rory, where are you? Rory, this isn't funny... come on." The young woman in the next stand searched under her table, then hurried between her tent and Helen's to scan the tall brown weeds and scrub brush that grew along a narrow strip behind the booths before the terrain lifted into a forested ridge. "Oh, my God.... *Ro-rry!*"

Meg, with Ethan on her heels, strode toward the woman as she rushed back.

"Chief! My son— I can't find my little boy. He's... oh, God, I don't know where he *went*."

"Easy, Lynette." Meg clasped the young woman's arms. "He can't have gone far. What was he wearing?"

Her eyes were frantic. "He was here one minute and then...then—"

"Deep breath. What's he wearing?" Meg repeated.

"A cowboy hat and a green sweatshirt and...and jeans."

"Sweatshirt got a picture on it?"

"That red car character from the movie *Cars*."

"I'll check the back area," Ethan said. "Sally, would you mind watching my mother's stuff?" he asked the dispatcher hastening across the aisle from her tent.

"Of course. You guys find little Rory."

The dispatcher's daughter-in-law called over, "Meg, I saw Rory playing between those tents about ten minutes ago."

Meg raised a hand in acknowledgment, then headed for the ribbon of weeds behind the booths. With her portable attached to the epaulet on her shirt, she called Gilby patrolling Cardinal Avenue. "Rory Alms, three years old, is missing from the fair." She relayed Lynette's description. "Get some volunteers to search the grounds and set up a road block on either end of Cardinal. He's probably playing in the dirt back here, but we can't take the chance it's not more serious."

A hundred feet ahead within the half-naked trees, a flash of blue told her Ethan had begun to comb the ridge. Meg walked slowly through the weeds. She followed the zigzagged crush of browned grass made by Ethan's boots along a thin trail of sprigs knocked aside by smaller feet.

In the woods, she sighed with relief when she heard his low rumbling voice intercepted by the high-pitched tone of a child.

Thank mercy.

Guided by the sounds, and climbing through a thick stand of ponderosa pine thirty feet in, she found Ethan on one knee beside Rory. Immediately she radioed Gilby the boy was safe.

"Hey, Rory," she said, understanding the gratitude for happy endings in Ethan's eyes. "Been having fun?"

"Uh-huh." His little fingers gripped a yellow toy bulldozer. "I builded lots of roads."

"That's great, buddy, but Mommy's looking for you."

"Uh-huh," he repeated. "Ethan said I be lost."

Crouching beside the child, Meg plucked a leaf from his tawny hair. "Ethan's right. But we'll get you back to Mom, okay?" She brushed dirt off one round cheek.

"Okay."

Meg took the dozer, then held out a hand to the child. Over his head her eyes met Ethan's. "Thank you," she mouthed.

With the boy between them, Ethan touched his lips to hers, and she felt the current of relief the kiss bore. "Told you we click," he said.

We click. She'd never had doubts in that department. At one time she and Ethan used to finish each other's sentences, and sense each other's moods with just a look. They had been in tune with each other's thoughts as if born identical twins. Pure and simple they were soul mates.

Key word, Meg. Were.

What about once soul mates, always soul mates?

Fantasy for the weak-kneed.

Life was about reality. Hadn't she learned that seven years ago?

Lifting the child into his arms, Ethan led the way out of the trees and across the easement of weeds, toward the fair's booths. Lynette stood with several commiserating women, one of them Helen, when Meg and Ethan walked from between the tents.

"Rory!" The mother rushed to take her son from Ethan's clasp. "Where have you been? I told you not to leave the tent. Didn't I?" Kisses against the child's hair muffled her rant.

"I'm sorry, Mommy. I builded lots and lots of roads with my dozer and then that mommy and daddy found me." The boy pointed to Meg and Ethan.

A tiny sting touched Meg's heart. Had life been different twenty years ago, she and Ethan might have been parents together.

Lynette hugged her son. "Thank you both," she said through a watery smile.

Meg nodded. Since she'd been a cop in Sweet Creek, they'd had two missing children during a community event. The first happened at the Fourth of July five years ago when a two-year-old wandered away from his parents' side while fireworks fizzed and crackled in the sky. The second occurred two years ago when a sixteen-year-old from Arizona visiting his grandparents' ranch got turned around in the bush on a coyote hunt. Meg never understood the necessity for children under eighteen handling guns. But this was Montana. And ranchers taught their children at a young age how to shoot—especially when it meant eliminating predators preying on their livestock.

Sally patted Lynette's shoulder, and Helen offered the young mother a blueberry muffin with a cup of coffee. "Sit and relax."

Ethan touched Meg's arm. "When was the last time you had something to eat?"

"Six-fifteen this morning." She glanced at the thin-banded watch on her wrist—2:12 p.m. The sound of raised voices swung her head around. "Just a minute."

She strode down the row to the fishing booth where the Brit had bought his rod and reel and where, momentarily, Jock Ralston's voice carried across the crowd gathering to watch and listen.

"Problems, Jock?" Meg stopped a few feet away.

"Nothing I can't handle," he retorted, tapping a fishing rod against his leg.

"Well, you seem a little agitated. Is there something I can help either of you with?"

"He won't pay my price," the gray-haired vendor complained. "And now he won't give back the rod."

Jock pointed to the bill on the table. "I gave him twenty for it. That's all this piece of junk's worth."

Meg sized up the rod; it appeared in excellent condition. "What's your price, Art?"

"Fifty." He glared at Jock.

"Can I have a look?" she asked, holding out her hand.

"What're you gawking at, Red Wolf?" Jock looked past Meg.

Ethan had come to stand beside her. "Need a hand?" he asked, ignoring the man and his scowl.

"Everything's under control, thanks," she told him, though her heart calmed in his presence.

"Take a hike, Red Wolf," Jock persisted. "This doesn't have anything to do with you."

"Jock," Meg interrupted. "May I see the fishing rod?"

He handed it over before folding his arms across his chest and planting his feet apart in a militant stance. "You can see it's not worth the fifty he wants."

She took her time examining the slim St. Croix rod and intricate reel, though she knew little about fishing poles. The two she had dealt with had been stolen from a sporting store and recovered within the day with the price tags still attached. This piece appeared as new as the stolen store tackle.

"I've only used it once. Two weeks ago," Art volunteered. "Caught a couple trout, but then my wife bought me a Premier for my birthday last weekend, that's why I'm selling this one."

"I'll give you fifty, Art." Ethan said and dug in his hip pocket for his wallet. "Can't get a rod like that under one-fifty."

"Just a second." Jock stepped between Meg and Ethan. "I had first dibs."

"You willing to pay the price?" Ethan asked mildly.

"I'm bargaining." Ralston grabbed the rod out of Meg's hands.

Ethan plucked it from Jock. "And I'm paying." He tossed down a fifty-dollar bill, which Art snatched up immediately.

"Sold," the vendor announced.

"You son of a bitch." Ralston slammed the butt of his hand against Ethan's chest. "You did that just to piss me off."

"Hold it." Meg insinuated herself between the two glowering men. "Are you willing to give Art his fifty, Jock?"

"No damned way."

"Then you've lost the sale, so I'm asking you to leave quietly and find something else to buy." Holding her breath she stared at him while he glared at Ethan. Had hatred been a blunt object, Jock Ralston would have used it on the man behind her.

"I'm not forgetting this, Tonto," he said. Spinning

around, he grabbed his twenty from the table and stormed off through the curious onlookers, an enraged Moses parting the Red Sea.

"You okay?" Ethan asked quietly as the mob slowly dispersed.

"Just peachy." After a nod to Art, Meg headed for the edge of the fairgrounds. "I owe you a thanks," she said when they were out of earshot.

"For what?"

"For buying that rod. I know how much you hate fishing." She cast him a glance. "What do you plan to do with it?"

"I don't know. Maybe use it for a still-life portrait."

Her lips bowed. "Which some avid sport fisherman will love to hang in his den."

"Huh. If he loves the price."

At that she laughed. Stepping onto the unusually crowded sidewalk, she said, "Seriously, thanks for helping with Art."

"Wasn't Art I was helping, Meggie."

It was her. "Appreciate it, anyway."

For several beats he said nothing. "I wish you weren't a cop. It's damned dangerous."

"Lots of jobs are dangerous."

"Not like police work. You put yourself in the face of it every time you deal with a situation."

"Is this going to be a problem for us, Ethan? Because if it is, then we need to stop before we ever begin." She halted under the spreading branches of a scarlet maple, hoping her expression meant business.

Their eyes held. Hard. Long. Her breath slowed. Around them the chatter ebbed—until they alone stood in the speckled sunshine of the tree.

"You haven't eaten since dawn," he said finally, breaking the trance.

"That isn't answering my question."

He set a hand on the small of her back, guided her across the street to the hole-in-the-wall called Cap'n Bligh's Sea. "I know, but I don't want to talk about it now. Feel like fish and chips?"

"Ethan—"

"Later, Meggie. I'm hungry."

She gave up—temporarily—called Gilby and told him she was taking an hour for lunch, but if anything arose to call her immediately. She left the same message with Pearl, their weekend dispatcher.

"Where's Beau?" Ethan asked.

"Making iced lattes, I hope." She scanned the tourists, checking unfamiliar faces and vehicles. This year the number appeared to be fewer—likely caused by the eradication of the annual Mounted Shoot Competition that always took place the next day on the former rifle range. The range Ethan was transforming into a riding retreat for troubled children.

"So he got the job at the coffee shop? That's great."

"We'll see. This is the first job that gives him an honest-to-God paycheck."

"Give him a chance, Meg."

She would. After the disaster with Doug, Beau had been quieter than normal, less confrontational, and he'd repaid the drinking and campfire misconduct on Ethan's property.

"What do you feel like?" he asked as their arms brushed.

"About a week's worth of sleep."

Concern filled his eyes. "I know just the place for a nap. But first, let's get a meal into you."

He bought two newsprint packages of fish and chips, and she paid for a pair of liter-size bottles of spring water. In his truck, she asked, "Where are we going?"

"My place. I figured we'd sit on the deck, enjoy a bit of quiet."

She rested her head against the seat. "A man after my heart."

"Always," he replied and drove out of town.

When he turned off the main road to take the one around the lake, Meg finally sneaked a peek across the cab. His mouth was stern, his eyes steady on the road, his hair blowing in the breeze from the open window.

She jerked back to reality. God, she had to stop romanticizing. Excluding that kiss, nothing would ever come of this...*thing* between them. Today, during their lunch, she would set the record straight, set the standard about them and about her work. In all the years she'd worked in Sweet Creek as chief of police, he'd never uttered his feelings concerning her position, not to her brother, not to anyone.

Of course not, Meg. Why would he?

Why indeed? Prior to these past few weeks she'd simply been a smidgen of his past. Yet, somehow, that idea felt false. She suspected she'd been in his thoughts as much as he'd been in hers.

He pulled into his yard, and Lila jumped up from the porch welcome mat to trot over, tail spinning hellos.

"Hey, old girl," Ethan greeted the dog as he climbed from the truck's cab. "Smell the goodies, do you? I'll save you a piece when we're done." Holding the lunch bag—and the new fishing rod—he rounded the hood to take Meg's hand and follow the path around the house to the rear deck. "What would you like to drink?" he asked. "I've got soda, too, or if you want a beer…"

"No beer while I'm working." She noted the bottled water in her hands. "This will do, thanks."

He went into the house while she walked to the edge of the deck. Since she'd seen his home the week before, someone had pruned the perennials in the planters and pots for winter. Ethan or Helen? she wondered. Helen had a green thumb, a trait that did not come naturally to Meg, much as she wished. She loved flowers and plants, but couldn't cultivate a sprig of elegance when it came to growing things from the soil.

Still, as always, a soul-deep peace washed through her. She could live here. She could make this house, this chunk of land home.

As long as Ethan lived here.

He brought out plates and napkins, set them on the small table joining the pair of Adirondack chairs. Flopping in one, he said, "Lunch is ready."

Suddenly exhausted, Meg walked to the remaining chair and lowered herself to its thick cushion. "This is the life," she said on a sigh. "I can't deny it."

He unwrapped the steaming fish. "You're welcome anytime, Meggie-girl. You know that."

"I do." She spread a napkin across her lap, then placed a chunk of fish onto a plate.

They ate in silence for several minutes. Lila lay at Ethan's feet, brown eyes watching each motion of his hands. Meg smiled. *He feeds her at the table.* Would she and Beau do the same with a dog, if they decided to obtain one from the SPCA? *Absolutely.*

Ethan wiped his fingers. "What you said about me

being a man after your heart is true. I am after your heart. I want us to begin again."

She leaned her head against the chair's cushion. "Is that why you brought me out here? To lull me into submission with these lovely surroundings?"

"Ah, my Meggie. You've never been a woman to be lulled into submission."

Closing her eyes briefly, she smiled. "At least you haven't forgotten that aspect of my nature."

"There's not much about you I've forgotten."

"Same here."

"What happened between us?"

She looked out at the water, unnaturally calm for late September when winds stole leaves from the trees. Soon the lagoon would be frozen and snow would cover Blue Mountain in quilts of white and the boulder across the water would shimmer like a massive diamond—so dissimilar to the spring day she had walked away from their relationship.

She said, "I was a coward about Farrah's problems." *I was a coward about your problem with Jock and Linc and wanted an excuse to escape the worry*. Ah, hindsight, the enlightener.

"So was I," he replied quietly. "Easier to ignore what was going on than deal with it."

"I wanted to tell the school counselor, but Farrah begged me not to tell anyone. She was so ashamed about being gay."

"Jock and Linc were bastards."

Meg turned her head. "They bullied you, too." *Jock is still playing Mr. Macho*. Today was a prime example.

Ethan shrugged. "They've never scared me." He shot her a grin. "I was bigger."

And he still was. But not their equal, not to them. Meg sighed. *Ah, Farrah, why didn't you let me help?* "I wish there was some way I could do something in her honor, you know?"

For a long time, he sat silent. At last, he said, "You can."

"How?"

"By telling parents of kids in trouble about the helping-horse stable I'm building."

"I thought it was for physically handicapped children."

"That, too. But I'd like to start with kids who are having trouble at school and/or at home. Kids like Farrah."

And you, she thought. While Helen had been a caring mother, he'd had to fight battles she knew nothing about. Racial battles that involved taunts and name-calling. Granted, only three kids had bullied him throughout those years, but that hadn't lessened the impact. So often she wished she could throw those same boys—now adults—behind bars.

One was Hudson Leland's son, Linc, the father of Randy. The other was Jock Ralston, father of the gun-popping Miles, who had sneered at Meg the night she and Ethan discovered the kids drinking around a camp-fire not four hundred yards from where she sat this instant. The last was Gilby, her second-in-command. As a senior he'd been a skinny, pimply kid needing atten-tion and acceptance, prime for manipulation by the likes of Jock and Linc. Fortunately, Gilby had grown up—and gained decency and wisdom.

Ethan continued, "Look at it this way. All those years came to some good." He took her hand and, in the middle of her palm, laid a kiss that rolled across her heart; she couldn't respond for the wedge in her throat.

Minutes later, he bundled up the remains of the fish and chips and took them into the house. When he came outside again, he held a three-foot mailing tube.

"Come, I want to show you something," he said, and went down the deck steps.

With a command to Lila to guard the house, he led Meg down a path that climbed up the wooded hill rising behind his shed. At the top they stopped to catch their breath.

The trail descended in a zigzag pattern through dense groves of pine, birch and spruce. Ethan led her carefully past rocky outcroppings and in and out of thick shadows and bright sunlight. Finally the trees thinned and she could see their destination. The old rifle range.

Except it was no longer the range where she had practiced her shot. The target mound had been leveled, and in its place lay several acres of flat terrain bordered by trees. At the heart of those acres was a partially built paddock and barn. The building's foundation had been laid, the walls framed, the roof done. A shell ready for completion.

"You built this since moving here?" she asked, stunned. *Since April?*

"Doesn't take long when you have good help." He smiled down at her. "Ash helped—and a few others—this summer."

Her brother. Ash would have rounded up a dozen people. As his foreman for years, Ethan had worked hours beyond his duty, hours Ash had not forgotten. Unfortunately, Ash would have kept his part in the construction quiet because of her history with the man beside her, because he'd known about their dreams.

"It's wonderful, Ethan," she said. Her chest felt inflated as a balloon. He'd followed their dream, the one they had talked about endlessly, the one she'd wanted to erect as a tribute to her wheelchair-bound stepfather.

Walking toward the barn, Ethan let go of her hand and slipped several blueprints from the mailing tube. Squatting on the ground near the open square that would become the big double doors, he spread out the first. "The horse barn and riding arena," he said. "I'm hoping to finish the building before the snow flies. At least enough that I can work out of the cold."

Meg crouched beside him. The barn and arena would accommodate twelve horses.

"Think the kids will like it?" His dark eyes searched hers.

She wanted to kiss him. For what he was doing with this bit of land, for the years he'd kept their dream alive and because he was so near she could see the gold specks in his irises and breathe the afternoon sun from his skin.

She recognized the instant he identified her desire. The query in his eyes altered.

"Meggie." Just her name. And a world of emotion. "I—" His voice, the one in a thousand fantasies, scraped along her flesh.

Thought, sense, logic. All flew with the autumn breezes whispering down the mountain. She leaned forward and set her mouth on his in a bold first move. The other kisses had come from him, this one was hers. She didn't care that she wore a uniform, that a gun was strapped to her belt, that a badge lay in her wallet. She didn't care that she should be back in town, ensuring its citizens were safe.

Ethan. His name swirled in her blood like warm wine.

Everywhere his hands touched. Her hair, along her jaw, down her arms. Pulling her closer and closer still—as if to slip her under his skin. Together they were a ballet of tongues and mouths and hands.

Somewhere in her mind she felt his fingers move to her broken breast—

A gunshot boomed down the mountainside.

"Get down!" Hand on her weapon, Meg slammed against Ethan, toppling him to the ground. The next second, his arms cocooned her and he rolled his body onto hers as a trio of pheasants, squawking and flapping, burst into the air at the far end of the field.

Meg almost laughed. Hunting season had started in a big way.

Then she remembered the No Trespassing signs posted on Ethan's land. Whoever hunted here had ignored his request. Clasped together, breath held, they lay stone still. She could feel his heartbeat thrashing against her breast. His eyes seized hers. *You okay?*

She was fine—if she forgot that he was on top of her and his legs bound her legs and her hips cradled his hips.

"Ethan, let me up," she whispered, moving to crawl out from under his big body. "I need to check—"

Determination in his eyes, he gripped her waist. "You're not going anywhere without me."

Three beats passed. Fighting him, she could see, was not an option. "All right. But keep close to me."

"I've always been close to you, Meggie. You just never knew it."

She hadn't. Not until this moment.

Chapter Ten

Ethan's heart whirled like a leaf in a hard wind.

Sitting up cautiously, Meggie said, "I want to see where that shot came from." She held up a hand when he opened his mouth about chasing a trigger-happy hunter. "Hear me out. Either the guy didn't see us and was actually aiming for the birds, or…he's making a hell of an effort to scare us. No matter how you look at it, he's not out to kill us."

"How can you be so sure?" Ethan wanted to know. If he had his way, he wouldn't allow her anywhere near a gun. Yeah, she knew how to shoot—he'd been at her side when they'd learned as kids—and, yeah, she was the police chief, which made her an expert shot, but out in the open…

She wasn't Superwoman. Her flesh bled like that of the six billion other people populating the earth.

"Had he wanted to hurt us—" she scanned the hillside "—we were perfect targets walking across the field."

"Fine, let's take a look." He'd walk out front. If the shooter wanted them dead, he'd go first, give her that split-second chance.

Mind in a turmoil, he strode ahead, legs chewing the distance to the trees. A picture formed in his mind, one in which he no longer wanted Meggie in her cop's job, a job where a sniper might have sat, waiting for them. Waiting for her.

Beneath the shelter of the forest, he watched her zig-zag back and forth, gun drawn, searching a fifty-foot radius around the lightning-downed tree he'd photo-graphed last month. The tree with its bird's-eye view of his stable. No, he didn't like her cop's job.

He found the spot where the tree's thick branches had been seared to nubs by lightning heat.

"Here," he called, picking up a twenty-two shell. An empty soda can dangled in a scraggly clump of fire-weed.

Meg hurried over. Bending at the waist, she exam-ined the site. "They were wearing hiking boots or some type of footwear that's conducive to walking in the bush. See the tread there." She pointed to several plain prints. "And here." With the pen from her shirt pocket, she nudged a cigarette butt. "Nonfilter. No lipstick."

Ethan rose. "Doesn't mean it's not a woman." Some women could be meaner than a witch's stick. His last relationship three years ago had nearly sent him moving out of state.

"You're right," Meggie said, pulling him back from a memory he'd rather forget. "But the size of that tread puts the odds in favor of it being a male." Hands on her hips, she surveyed the incline, the woods. "Let's see if we can follow a trail."

They found another footprint about seventy feet to the left. The culprit had headed back to the cut line curving around the hill to join Lake Road past Ethan's riding retreat.

In the distance a motor fired. They broke into a run, dodging trees as the ground rose and fell over two dry creek beds.

Ethan reached the road five paces ahead of Meggie. "Goddamn it," he panted.

"Could be he's spooked. Him running doesn't mean the shot was planned and deliberate."

She stood close enough for him to catch another whiff of the jasmine shampoo she preferred. "And this should make us feel good? Jeez, woman. Next time his aim might find a true mark."

Her pupils narrowed to chips of blue. "There won't be a next time, Ethan. I'll find this guy before that happens."

"And if you don't?"

She stared at the tire tracks in the dirt. "Oh, trust me. I will."

"Let me help."

She shook her head. "I've been a cop for six years. It's my problem."

In other words, she'd dealt with scum and survived—without him. What made him think she needed him now?

Trouble was, he wanted her to need him. *The way you need her.*

Hell. In damn near twenty years he hadn't needed a woman to enrich his life, to make it complete or whatever mumbo jumbo psychologists loved to herald when it involved the human species.

The difference was Meggie.

For him, it had always been about her.

His insides churned as she radioed Gilby Pierce on her portable. The hunt had begun in earnest.

After Ethan dropped her off at the office—with barely a brush of his mouth on hers—Meg grabbed her camera and returned to the trail where the shooter had parked his vehicle in the dirt. Back at the station, she attached the photos in an e-mail with a quick note to Rolf, her contact at the lab in Billings, requesting the make and size of the tire. Thirty-five minutes later, Pearl, the weekend dispatcher, put a call through to Meg's office. It was Rolf.

"Got a possible make on that tire tread you wanted, Meg," he said without preamble. "Looks like it could've been laid down by a Michelin Latitude X-Ice."

"X-Ice?" Meg clicked open her e-mail to retrieve the photos she had sent. "Sounds like a winter tire."

"Yep. *If* this is your tire, it's put on pickups, SUVs and vans for extreme winter conditions. Considering October's three days away, your perp is about a month early. But here's what you should be looking for—left back tire has a nick in it."

Meg studied an enlarged photo. "What kind of nick?"

"Look at photo number two. See that little black spot to the bottom right of the tread?"

"I see it."

"That's a nick. He's run over something sharp like a piece of glass or metal and took out a tiny chunk of rubber. If you look at photo seven, it's there again. Bet if you go back to the scene, you'll see it approximately every four feet."

"I will. Thanks, Rolf."

"Anytime, Chief."

After setting down the receiver, she grabbed her keys from her desk drawer.

"Be back in a half hour, Pearl."

On the trail where she and Ethan saw the shooter drive away, Meg got out of the police pickup. Rolf was right. Barely visible in the dirt, the notch was there like the quarter hour on a clock.

Returning to Sweet Creek, she slowed at Ethan's lane. Had he gone home after dropping her off? He hadn't been pleased with her decision not to allow him to help her with this case.

She should turn in, explain that she could not have him endangering his life—if things got worse. A shiver traced her skin at the thought of something happening to Ethan.

God forbid.

And suddenly it hit. All the years she had avoided him. All the years she'd consciously blocked her mind and heart to communication, to amend the rift, *to try again,* he'd been *there.*

A wake of wasted years trailed her life. And then…

He'd been first to step up to the plate of reconciliation, first to voice the words "I want to see you."

To kiss her.

Despair. It flooded through her with such force she pulled to the side of the road to catch her breath. Gripping the wheel, she stared into the tree-canopied lane leading down to his house. *Ethan.*

She wanted him back in her life. She wanted to start anew. But, *Lord,* could she get past her insecurities?

Could she take the chance he would judge her?

A walnut-size knot leaped into her throat. Her heart bonged against her breastbone. In her lungs the air thinned.

Breathe, Meg. Do the steps. Slow and steady. It's okay. You're having a panic attack. Nothing you haven't dealt with in the past four years. You'll be fine. Just a couple minutes…

Panic attacks that started after Mark, who had been okay with her reconstruction but questioned the nursing value "of only a single real breast."

Deliberately, she loosened her fingers on the wheel, placed them over her mouth and breathed deep, extending her stomach as she inhaled. Closed her eyes. *Think positive…. Think of Beau….*

When her heart quieted and the block behind her tongue dissolved, she slipped the truck in gear and drove past Ethan's entrance and back to town.

By five o'clock the sun arranged an array of color along the crest of Blue Mountain. In Sweet Creek, the parking lot and grounds behind the courthouse were empty, and the sidewalks on Cardinal Avenue sported almost no foot traffic. Shop owners had placed their Closed signs in the windows in preparation for Sunday. Harvest Moon Dayz tourists had retired to nearby campgrounds or traveled back to their residences in neighboring towns.

Through the impending dusk, Meg looped the streets one last time, ensuring her town was safe and no bandits hung around for unsavory purposes.

With an enlarged photograph of the tire tread on the

passenger seat, she drove slowly through the four blocks of residential streets, noting trucks, vans and SUVs. Beginning Monday, she would send Gilby on a daily foot patrol around town. Chances they'd find the exact tire were slim, but at this point, she was not about to shelve the case as an open-ended file.

As she turned the last corner onto Robin Road, Sweet Creek's only dead-end street, she saw Hudson Leland standing beside a blue Taurus parked in front of his house. The driver wore a straw cowboy hat. As she approached, he looked over his shoulder.

The Brit from the craft fair.

When she pulled beside the rental, his passenger window rolled down. "Evening, Chief McKee."

She nodded. "Evening, gents. Recruiting new residents, are you, Mr. Mayor?"

He laughed heartily. "We can always use new blood in the town, as you know. Unfortunately, Roland, here, lives in California."

"Really? What brings you to our dot on the map, Mr. Roland?"

"Actually, Roland is my first name. Carleton is my last name."

"*Dr.* Carleton," Hudson boasted.

She reined in surprise. She'd pegged him a businessman of the shady sort. "A little out of your jurisdiction, aren't you, Doctor?" Or did physicians in surfer land normally tour flea markets?

"I came up with a couple colleagues to hunt Montana's beautiful and rugged wilderness." He offered a dazzling grin she'd bet her salary was entirely porcelain.

"What sort of hunting?"

"Oh, mostly water fowl, as well as a few quail."

How about pheasants or eagles? "Are you a sport hunter?"

His ears reddened. "Truth be known, I've never shot any bird."

"Ah." She let the single sound settle. "So your aim is off."

"Well, no—"

"Meg," Hudson interjected. "Doc Carleton's my guest. It's not necessary to grill him about something that Montana is famous for." He chortled. "Our chief isn't a fan of hunting—unless it's bad guys."

Carleton drummed his fingers on the steering wheel. "The only kind that matters."

Meg studied Leland. He seemed edgy. "Sorry for the offense, Mayor. Our craft fair tends to bring people from all over, so when an unfamiliar face stays past closing time, it's my job to ensure that it's for the best reasons."

"Can't agree more," Carleton said. "Wish it were the same in Sacramento."

Sacramento? Was this one of Doug's colleagues? "What kind of work do you do, Roland?" she asked.

He laughed. "All sorts. I practice with the best."

She raised her eyebrows. "That must be rewarding."

"It is. Dr. Sutcliffe is incredible."

Meg kept her breathing even. "That's good to hear. Who you work with can certainly affect your career." She sent both men a smile. "Well, good night, gentlemen."

"'Night, Meg," they said in unison.

She put the truck in Reverse and pulled around to head back the way she'd come. At the station, she dialed Doug's cell phone.

He picked up on the second ring. "Dr. Sutcliffe."

"It's Meg."

A second's pause. "Marjorie! I was just thinking about you…and Beau."

Beau, the afterthought. She wanted to yank her ex-husband through cyberspace. "Look, something's come up and I need to know the names of your colleagues in Sacramento."

A pause. "Why?"

"It's important, Doug, or I wouldn't be asking."

He named four. Carleton wasn't one.

"Did you ever, at any time, work with a Roland Carleton?"

"Roland Carleton? I worked *on* him, not with him. He was a patient of mine last spring."

Camera in hand, Ethan closed the door of his studio. For a long minute he stood on the stoop, simply enjoying the massive harvest moon trailing a golden swath of light across the lagoon. He'd noticed the lunar sight through the window and remembered he had marked this night on the calendar for photos. But his mind had been full of Meggie….

Throwing herself over him when that shot rang out.

Determined to investigate the case without him.

Silent and resolute in the truck as he drove her back to the police station.

And let's not forget that kiss by my barn.

He took a deep breath, tasting her again, his skin vibrating to the memory. He had to stop thinking about her—or miss his deadlines. His achy shoulders from today's marathon sketching and printing session, seventy cards in six hours, warned him to refocus.

On the path Lila looked back and whined.

"I know. You think I'm crazy, but at least they're done."

Ethan headed for the house. Tomorrow morning, he'd call his friend and owner of the Seattle card outlet selling his work, tell him the lot would be in the mail Tuesday.

He fed Lila, patted her side. "Sorry for letting you starve, old girl. It won't happen again."

The moon beckoned. Pictures evolved in his mind. Sensual, sultry pictures. *Meggie in the moon.*

Ethan tugged on a fleece-lined vest. Snatching a granola bar and an apple off the counter, he went out the back door, Lila on his heels.

"Stay," he told the canine. "Guard the house." Tonight he would not risk leaving his home and studio without Lila's presence.

Down at the pier, he climbed into the Merrimack, and silently paddled through the quiet waters along the shoreline to the mouth of the dry creek bed, the natural border between his property and Meg's. There he hauled the canoe ashore.

Sometimes a man had to do what a man had to do when a beautiful woman was on his mind.

And Meggie, you've been there for thirty years. It's time we did something about it.

Chapter Eleven

A block of light fell from her kitchen window and the second back room he assumed was her bedroom. Since he came from the creek and approached the house at its right side, he saw her truck parked in front of the single-car garage. Beau's pickup was not home.

She was alone.

Ethan hesitated. Now that he was here, apprehension rose.

Would she be willing to come into the night with him, or would she stay in the warmth of her house and wait for her son?

Would she think him foolish, asking her onto the water after that shot this afternoon?

Years ago he could have asked her anything, taken her anywhere—at anytime. But this was a bold and independent Meggie. She worked a man's job, carried a gun and broke up fights and tracked down criminals.

But she kissed you like a woman. Like no *other* woman.

Holding on to that memory, he stepped away from the trees, crossed the yard and went up the porch steps. He knocked three times on the weathered wooden door. Deep in the darkness of the mountain, a wolf howled.

Ethan was about to knock again when a chain jingled. Opening the door a crack, she peered above six-inches of brass links.

"It's me," he said.

Immediately she unlatched the chain, swung the door wide. "Sorry, I didn't see a vehicle…. Come in."

"I walked. And should've called."

Backlit by the soft lamplight beside the couch, she looked small and fragile in tan jeans and a rosy top— and bare feet. Toes unvarnished. His sensible Megs.

Shutting the door behind him, she took in the camera around his neck and her lips twitched. "Out taking pictures of the moon?"

"Beau home?"

"He's out with friends. Why?"

Ethan wanted to pull her into his arms, tuck her safely against his heart. "Come out in the canoe with me."

Surprise flashed. "Right now?"

"Now's the best time. Come see the moon with me, Meggie."

Their eyes held. He watched her swallow—and understood her nerves. The night, the moon. Just the two of them under its spell.

"You're serious," she said.

"Wouldn't be here if I wasn't." He tried a grin, faltered. "It's a beautiful night. Won't get many more like it."

She took a deep breath. "Well, they say full moons cause people to go a little crazy."

This time he could grin. "Wanna go a little crazy together?"

She laughed. "Let me get my coat."

"And some socks and boots," he called as she headed for the kitchen, her small bare heels the sexiest sight he'd seen in years.

When she returned, she had on a silver bomber jacket, hiking boots and a mint-green scarf around her neck. In her hands, was a pair of gloves the same color as the scarf.

"All set?" she asked, her smile impish.

He nearly tugged her forward by the scarf and kissed her, but held off. If he touched her now, they would never get out the door and the moon would fade with the stretch of night.

He led her through the woods, down the creek bed, to the dark shoreline and the canoe on the grass. He offered her the extra life preserver before tugging on his own. After sliding the craft to the water, he settled her in, then took the paddle and pushed off.

The water lay still, glossed in silver and gold from the moon. Ripples lapped outward as he paddled the little green canoe slowly toward the middle of the lagoon.

He could envision the photo already. Her silhouetted within the orangey-gold sphere between the peak of Blue Mountain and the distant Absarokas rising to the east. Her eyes took in the beauty of the night: the golden sheen of water, the shadowy stands of shoreline trees, the hulking mass of hills and above them, the star-sugared sky.

The cool September breeze danced through her hair, fluttering a strand against her mouth, and for an instant he let the canoe glide while he reached forward to brush the lock away. Clasping the paddle, he resumed stroking through the water. But her eyes caught his and he could not look away.

"Where are you taking me?" she asked in a hushed voice.

"Where would you like me to take you?"

For a long moment she remained silent. "Where isn't important. It's how we get there that is."

And he knew they no longer spoke of canoe rides. "The journey," he said, "will be gentle and very, very fine, my Meggie. Trust me on that."

She looked away, her profile eggshell pale in the obscurity. "Can I?" Her eyes wove back to him. "Trust you?"

Something slipped into his gut. Something that had nothing to do with what he felt for her, and everything about what he sensed in the turn of her head, the unspoken words between them.

A lack of confidence.

The notion broke his heart. "You can," he murmured. "From here on."

Again her gaze latched onto his. "Ethan, I'm really not the same person you knew."

"You've told me that, babe." *Twice.* "But whatever it is that's scaring you, we'll get by it."

"Who said I'm scared?"

Resting the paddle across the gunwales, Ethan let the craft drift down the watery pathway of orange moonlight. He removed her clenched hands from her lap and warmed them with his own. "You wouldn't keep insisting you've changed if you weren't uneasy about what I might discover."

Again the averted look. "There's nothing to discover."

For a moment he hesitated. Something had happened to her since their teenage days, and that something had hurt her deeply. Once she'd been a funny, carefree young woman, ready to become a lawyer, eager to begin saving money for their "healing horses." In those days he would not have pictured her a cop, living to the letter with rules and laws, investigations and criminals—and caution as her sidekick.

Something had altered her point of view, driven her to deal with the nasty side of society rather than the hopeful faces of youth. "What happened between you and your husband, Meggie?"

Ethan's question had Meg trembling. She could not explain her mastectomy. *Could not*. "Doug wanted something I wasn't able to give him. End of story."

"He cheated." Not an inquiry, but a conclusion.

"In a way, yes."

"Is there any other way?"

"It had nothing to do with a woman or—" she cast Ethan a sideways look "—another man." Instead, he had cheated her out of the support she'd needed from a spouse, her committed lifelong partner. *Through sickness and health*. He'd deterred from the sickness part. "Doug's a perfectionist," she said, glad of the dark and that true feelings could hide within it.

"And you couldn't live up to his expectations."

"Something like that."

"Bastard."

She shrugged with a nonchalance she didn't feel. "Win some, lose some."

"Next time he's in town, let me know."

At that she chuckled. "And then I'd have to toss you in jail."

He picked up the paddle again, dipped in once, twice. "Wouldn't be the first time."

"You?" she asked, astounded. "When were you in jail?" Ash, her brother, had never mentioned a word.

"Happened a couple years after we broke up." Again, Ethan let the craft cruise slowly. "This should be about right. Turn your head left, look up at the mountain." He lifted his camera to his eye, adjusted the lens.

"How long were you in jail?" she asked, compelled to ask. Compelled, considering she was the law.

"Six months. I'd knocked a guy unconscious in a bar. Don't move. That's it...."

The camera clicked and whined and flashed, over and over.

"Okay, that's enough." She turned and faced him. "Why did you knock him out?"

"He was choking his wife because she'd danced with me. And, no, we weren't having an affair—although that's what he claimed to the judge."

"And he believed the husband?"

"Yep. I was just a drunken Indian. Except I'd only had one beer. The husband had downed a couple six-packs. Enough to have the bartender cut him off."

She could see the entire ordeal play out in her mind, aching for him because sometimes the law turned on the Good Samaritan. "And he didn't go to jail."

Ethan lifted his camera and clicked off another shot. "What do you think?"

She couldn't respond. She knew. Someone had to do time and Ethan had been the fall guy. Some judges she wanted to slap silly.

"Didn't the police do a Breathalyzer test?"

"Sure. But the couple was from one of those generational ranching families in Wyoming, and the judge an old-time friend on the husband's side. Which I didn't find out until after I was released."

He laid the paddle in the hull and they drifted toward the pier he and Beau had repaired. She'd been so engrossed in visions of Ethan at that bar, dancing innocently with a woman, then landing in jail for no other reason than he was a stranger with no connections, that she hadn't noticed they'd circled the lake's shoreline and returned home.

He caught the rope around the pylon and secured the canoe to the wood. Lila trotted out from under the weeping willow to stand wriggling on the pier.

"Hey, girl. Miss us?" Ethan climbed from the craft and Meg waited a moment while he gave the dog an affectionate pat before holding out his hand to her. "She generally comes along," he said.

"And tonight I took her place," Meg put in.

He pulled her close, nuzzled her hair. "Lila's not the jealous type."

"I'm glad," she whispered. "Did you get enough pictures?"

"I could take a million of you and they wouldn't be enough."

He studied the moonlight on the water before leading her to the end of the dock near the willow tree. "Right here."

"What?"

"Take off your jacket and scarf. I promise it won't take long."

She removed her outerwear, tossed it onto the wood several feet away.

"See where the moon is?" Her shoulder between his hands, he turned her to face the lagoon.

Meg looked across the water. The moon hung like an orange medieval shield a short distance above the horizon.

Ethan turned her again. "Stand sideways, like this. Now, lean back and put your hands in your hip pockets."

Meg knew the image she would present. A profile of her body, of her face and torso. Of her breasts. "I can't, Ethan. This isn't…" *Me.*

"It's shadow and light, babe. That's all I'm seeing."

"You're seeing my…" Breasts.

"I'm seeing the female body," he countered, "in a silhouette of night light." He cupped her cheek. "This is just for me, Meggie. No one else."

"You won't put the pictures on a calendar or some card?"

"You," he said, fiercely, "are not for sale." His eyes gripped hers. "Ever."

She relaxed a little. "All right."

He stamped a kiss on her lips, stepped away. After examining and realigning her position, he crouched and raised the camera, adjusted the lens. "Let your head fall back slowly. That's it, honey. Perfect. Hold right there." The camera clicked. "Beautiful. So beautiful."

His quiet, low words sent a thrill through Meg. For the first time in years, she felt…could it be? *Could* this feeling be…*wanton?* When had she felt this excited? This *normal?*

She thought of those dark eyes watching her, observing her pose, skimming the line of her body, her shape and curves, and her heart drummed in her chest. On a surge of bravado she arched her spine, tilted her head to strike her sexiest pose. She wanted to fling off her clothes, stand before him naked with the moon's glow brushing her flesh.

"Meggie." His voice rasped and she closed her eyes and smiled. She was woman. *I can roar.* At last. *At last.*

His palm cupped her cheek, warm skin on cool. "My Meg," he whispered before his mouth found hers, and her arms wrapped his neck and she was lost in him.

This kiss was as none previous. He took and she gave. Gentleness spun into a need so fierce she thought she would die if she didn't have him, here on the boardwalk, under the harvest night.

Her hands were in his hair. She wanted him wrapped around her body, and pressed closer, and closer still, recognizing the blatant fullness of him against her stomach as his hands, those restless hands ran up her sides, fingers seeking softness and curvature....

With a groan, Meg wrenched her mouth from Ethan's. "No. No," she said again, gasping air. Her forehead dropped to his chest. "We have to stop. This is too fast."

He kissed the top of her head. "It won't go anywhere you don't want it to, Meggie."

She moved to gather up her jacket and scarf. "That's the trouble. I *do* want. I want you so much I think I'll jump out of my skin if we don't do it."

He came to her, helped tug on the coat, set the scarf around her neck. "We'll do it when you're ready."

She stared up at him. "You're okay with waiting?"

A slow, slanted smile. "Honey, it's been twenty years, what's a week or two more? This is too important for both of us not to feel completely at ease."

Her eyes stung. "I never should have walked away from you that day."

"No regrets, Meggie." He lifted her chin with a work-hardened knuckle. "We're together now. It's all that matters. Come on, I'll take you home in the truck."

Thirty minutes later in the studio, he downloaded the photos from the camera onto the computer. Five dozen shots in all, but the last batch, the last eleven, were incredible.

She stood haloed by the moon. The dock lay in shadow and light at her feet, the water glinted silver and gold behind her, while the hills jutted their silhouettes into the glittering night sky.

But Meggie staged each frame. Her lithe and lanky frame in that formfitting rose-colored top with its tiny cup sleeves and those tight tan jeans. Her arms were bare, their long, fine bones bending out from her backside as she kept her hands in her hip pockets. A hint of moonlight shone in the minuscule triangle formed by her arms.

But it was the light streaming along the edge of her profile, down her thin neck to the tips of her breasts, then flowing in a long, elegant line along her tummy and thighs that held him in awe.

At the juncture where thigh met her femaleness, he could almost make out the slight convex/concave contours.

And if he let his imagination tarry, he could envision the gossamer paleness of her skin—on the length of her leg, the jut of her hip, the arc of her breast, the angle of her shoulder.

She had perfect proportions. Implicitly sensual and

sexy. Yet there was a mystery to her he could not describe. She was the goddess of night and dreams— and the girl next door.

I want you so much I think I'll jump out of my skin if we don't do it.

Except tonight she had fled. From his embrace, his kiss, his touch. And it hadn't been the first time. "What is it," he asked the photo on the screen, "that scares you about our kisses?" *About me.*

Staring at her outline, he backtracked in his mind, re-membering each moment she had rushed out of his arms and away. His hands had touched there and there and there, but not...*there*—

He sat back in his chair, eyes narrowed on the line that made her most female in the profile.

She had not wanted him to touch her breasts.

Doug's a perfectionist.

As a plastic surgeon the man would need to be a perfectionist.

Ethan studied the photo, the precision of lines. Whenever he touched her breasts, she put a halt to their kissing.

Why, Meggie? Did you have a breast alteration? As a teenager, he estimated her a C-cup.

Or had her fear derived from something else? A shiver tripped down his spine. *She's okay. There's nothing wrong.*

At least, not in the years she had been a cop. He had to hold on to that fact. Hell, she'd bowled him over on the ground, out by his half-built barn, chased a hunter through a quarter mile of mountain bush. He closed Adobe, shut down the computer.

No more secrets, Meg. That's what got us into trouble the last time.

And Ethan had no intention of letting the past repeat itself.

She sat on the edge of her bed and stared into the dresser mirror. She'd taken off her clothes except for her bra and panties.

Bit by bit, she inched off the bra, looked at her flesh, at the slant and bow of one, then the other.

He had caressed her *there.* Just for a second.

And she had let him, knowing he didn't suspect.

Of course, he wouldn't. Looking as she was now, there was no difference—*if* you didn't know. But *she* did. She could see the slight enlargement of the one, the way it formed toward her arm. She could see the tiny pinprick tattoos, billboard signs of her ordeal.

She reached for the clobetasol cream, the cream the doctor had prescribed years ago to apply in order to minimize the redness, the scarring. Seven years and the difference hadn't altered. Yet she applied the cream every night. Useless, but a ritual she could not give up. Because Doug had measured the surgery with analytical eyes and believed he could have done better. Mark had measured her "problem" as he called it, according to her ability to nurture babies.

How would Ethan measure her?

Tonight he had seen her as a woman, ripe and willing and full of desire to mate. She had danced a mating dance there on his wooden pier. She had wiled her female skills, tossing back her head, exposing herself against the light of the moon.

And he had wanted her. She'd seen it in his eyes, felt

it thrum through his body. And, heaven help her, she had wanted him.

Face it, Meg. You've always wanted him.

Marrying Doug on the rebound had been her second mistake. Going to college with the intent of finding a man who would want her without parameters, without the baggage of suicidal best friends or childhoods steeped in culture discrepancies, had been her worst mistake.

But she had been angry. And lost.

And so damned heart sore.

Every night for four months she had cried over Ethan. When she'd heard he left town without a word, she had gone to college, reasoning she would get a career and move on. But when she heard he was dating another woman not six weeks after they broke up, Meg crumpled onto the floor of the room she shared with another student and cried until she was sick. He'd been her friend, her love since she was seven years old and he eight, and six weeks after she walked away he was dating someone else.

How could she have made such a mess of their love? *How could he?* They were soul mates.

Weren't they?

Apparently not. And so, she went on the hunt: dated, partied, danced until dawn, smoked a little pot. In a year and a half she had three flings before she met Doug.

In the mirror her eyes appeared bruised. She *had* loved Doug, though not as she'd loved Ethan. Perhaps that incongruity—marrying a man she did not love in the forever kind of way—had been her greatest failing.

The saving grace was Beau. Doug had given her a child to cherish and hold and shower with all the love stored in her heart.

She gazed at her breasts, one true, one fake. Sixteen years ago she'd been whole, able to feed Beau with her body. Four years ago, Mark questioned that ability and she'd kicked him out.

Thirty-six meant her biological clock ticked the days into the past. Still, her childbearing years were far from over. Women in their forties had babies. Given her normal cycle, *and* if the cancer never returned, she might have eight years in which to give birth again.

Question is, Meg, with this body would you want another baby?

Yes! She sucked at her trembling lips, inhaled hard. *Yes, God help me, I do.*

The instant she'd locked on to Ethan's earthy eyes in her office three weeks ago, the thought of another baby had filled her daytime dreams while the one of Ethan coming to her out of the woods dressed in Native American regalia had woken her an hour before dawn on three separate occasions. Each identical. Each voicing the exact words: *I've never left you.*

Except for the last dream.

The one in which he'd replied, *We've never left you.*

We. She recalled her bewilderment in that final dream. *We?*

And reaching back, he'd tugged into view a tiny girl in a yellow dress and long black pigtails.

Instantly the dream had snapped closed and Meg shot awake. "Ariana," she'd whispered, her throat thick with tears.

Ariana.

The name they had chosen as teenagers for their first daughter.

Swallowing back the memory, Meg rose, slipped

from her underwear and reached for the oversized T-shirt draped over the foot rail. "You're a cop for God's sake," she said to the reflection in the mirror. "You deal in logic, common sense, the guts of life."

Dreams were fanciful fluff, the brain having a bit of nighttime recreation. She crawled under the covers. Took up the novel on the bedside table. Opened the pages. Checked her clock—11:22 p.m.

Another hour and Beau's curfew would bring him home. She would read until her *real-life* baby walked through the kitchen door and crept to his room.

Ariana.

Fluff and stuff. She forced herself to focus on the novel.

Chapter Twelve

Her cell phone rang Sunday morning as she sat in her robe at the kitchen table eating a toasted bagel and reading Sweet Creek's *Rocky Times*. Her sister-in-law, Rachel, had once worked for the newspaper—until Ash had fallen crazy in love with her and taken Rachel and her little boy to the ranch.

Rising from her chair, Meg smiled at the notion of big broody Ash falling for a reporter—though Rachel wrote nonfiction books now, between being a wife and a mother to their ten-month-old daughter and two older children.

"McKee," she said into the phone.

"Gilby here, Chief."

Her smile dropped. Gilby never called on a Sunday, her day off, unless there was a significant problem. "What's up?"

"We've got graffiti on Cardinal. They hit every business."

The stove clock read 8:11 a.m. Sweet Creek's commerce, what there was of it, was closed on Sunday. "Any complaints yet?"

"Not yet. Nobody around this time a day."

There wouldn't be; on Sunday, Cardinal Avenue lay deserted until it was time for the ten-o'clock services at the tiny, white steepled church sitting on the northern periphery of town.

"The mayor will need to be informed," she stated, her imagination conjuring the mess community services would need to clean. "I take it the real estate office was included in the spree?" These days, along with the mayor's position, Leland sold real estate with his son, Linc.

"No one was spared."

She sighed. "No doubt I'll be hauled on the carpet about it tomorrow." No more than she planned to do to the man himself, concerning *Dr.* Roland Carleton, whom she was investigating through California channels. "Meet me at the office in twenty."

She hung up. Graffiti in urban areas was commonplace, and Sweet Creek received its share on yard fences, garage doors and Dumpsters. This was different. This, however, reeked of more than a prank. This was maliciousness down to the core.

Gulping down her leftover bagel, Meg hurried into the shower. After checking out the scene of the crime, she'd pay a visit to the mayor to discuss the damage— and the illusive Roland Carleton.

Five minutes later, with towel-dried and finger-combed hair, she tossed on a green sweater and a pair of jeans, left a note for Beau, then headed out to her Silverado.

The mess confronted the eye as she turned off Lake Road onto Cardinal Avenue. The first building was Innis Insurance, its door, window and wall space scrawled in yellow spray paint. Across the street, Klever Kids Klothing was equally marred. *Senseless scribbling,* Meg thought, unable to distinguish a rhyme or pattern to the confusion. For two blocks each store and business stared at her with defaced windows and walls. The trail wound from one building to the next without a break, like a tangle of long yellow snakes.

At the end of the last block, she pulled to the curb and got out of her vehicle. Striding around the hood, Meg zeroed in on what appeared to be the first sign of lettering under the tail of the paint's path on the window of the Hair Do salon.

"This is Eew." *This* and *is* were exact and distinct. Not so with the three final letters. E-e-w. Eew as in gross? Or had someone signed his or her initials? No matter, it was a start. She flipped open her cell phone, called Gilby. "Meet me at the Hair Do."

"Got something?"

"Maybe."

"I'm there."

True to his word, she saw her second-in-command step from the station a block and a half away. He jogged toward her.

"What do you make of this?" she asked, pointing to letters on the salon's feature window.

Resting a hand on his gun belt, Gilby leaned in for

a closer look. "Initials maybe. Or were you thinking something else?"

"Ditto on the initials, which means we need to track down an E.E.W. in our system. Worst-case scenario, we'll need to start checking the phone book."

"E-e-w?" Again Gilby bent to the script. "Or e-r-w?

Shoulder to shoulder with her officer, Meg examined the letters. "Hmm. The way the second letter loops like an *r* and the *w* is half finished… Could be an exaggerated *r* running into the *w.*"

She straightened. *This is Erw.* E-R-W. A memory wavered in the shadows of her mind. Something familiar. Where had she seen the initials before? "What time did you shut down last night?"

"Ten. Place was dead."

She nodded. "Mayor's going have a fit. He'll want this cleaned up and taken care of within the next twenty-four hours. Isn't going to happen, though." She looked down the street where a cold first-of-October wind whipped tiny whirlwinds of dust and leaves. "I need you to work the street this morning, check with Alice upstairs here." She pointed to the curtained apartment above the salon where the owner lived. "And Old Joe above his bakery and Ralph and Lou down at Toole's Ranch Supplies. See if anyone heard or saw anything suspicious."

"Got it." Gilby started for the back door of the salon and the outside stairs to Alice's apartment. "I'll let you know if something comes up."

"Yep, and Gil…?"

He paused, eyes squinting against the wind.

"Thanks. You're doing a heckuva job."

With a thumbs-up, he grinned. "Same at ya, Chief."

Meg climbed into her truck. In her office at the station, she went through the computerized database of victims, complainants and arrests she'd compiled since beginning her career in Sweet Creek. No one with first and middle names E.R. under the Ws.

She shut down the computer, grabbed her jacket off the hook behind the door. Stepping into the corridor, she glanced into the empty interview room across the hall. Would she ever pass the spot without thinking of Ethan sitting there sketching out his statement?

In that room, she had known she was in trouble. His eyes had seen *her* for the first time in years, and they'd tugged at a truth she could no longer deny. She had loved him all her life.

Last night she could have slept with him. All she'd needed to do was say *yes,* one word, one three-lettered word, and he would have led her to his bed. *To him.*

Three-letters: *E.R.W.*

Ethan Red Wolf.

Heart pounding, she stared into the interview room. Spinning on her heels, she rushed into the records room, to the filing cabinet housing hundreds of hardcopy complaints and statements.

Under the *R*s she found the page of sketches. Hauling the sheet from the file, she scrutinized the signature filling the bottom corner.

Ethan Red Wolf.

E.R.W.

Had the culprit intended to frame him?

On the statement, each letter pointed deeply to the right, as if they stood in a blizzard wind. The signature on the windowpane of the Hair Do dragged in a rounded, vertical format. The way Beau wrote. With the careless simplicity of youth.

Doesn't mean a thing.

But I have to check all the angles, eliminate any and all possibilities. A flush of shame heated her cheeks.

For the first time she hated her job. Hated that it made her suspicious and wary and cynical. That, damn it, she had to check out the people she loved.

Like Beau.

And Ethan. And not a minute after she pictured herself in his bed. It made her sick to think she had to check his signature. Just to make sure.

Returning the statement to its folder, she closed the filing cabinet. *Go home, Meg. Let Gilby handle this one. It's graffiti, not murder.* She strode out the back door to her truck, climbed behind the wheel and was almost out of town when she glanced right, toward Robin Road. *What the hell,* no sense putting off until tomorrow what she could do in the next few minutes.

She swung down the street, intent on the mayor's sprawling blue-and-white Craftsman home. Of course, the "doctor's" rental was nowhere in sight, as it hadn't been after she'd talked to Doug and retraced her route through town. Not ten minutes between the time she'd talked to Carleton, then Doug, had Hudson Leland's "friend" slunk away like a rat in a garbage pile.

Pulling into the bricked driveway, Meg killed the engine. *Let's see what you've got to say for yourself, Mr. Mayor.*

"Glad you're here, Meg," Leland said when he opened the front door. "What the hell's going on up-town? Just got a call from Gilby."

"We're on it, Mayor. At the moment, Officer Pierce is checking with the residents on Cardinal."

He snorted. "You honestly think Old Joe heard or saw those hooligans? Old fart goes to bed at eight."

"There are other residents," she pointed out. He hadn't invited her inside, but kept himself in the doorway. Which meant he had company. Question was, who? And were they male or female?

Female, Meg could rationalize. Hudson Leland was in his late-fifties and aging well, and he'd been divorced for twelve years. Though his hair had thinned, it still maintained its brown color, and while his eyebrows could use a trimming, beneath them, his irises were a charming hazel.

"Another thing," she said, keeping her eyes steady on his face. "I'm wondering why Mr. Carleton lied about his profession."

The shaggy brows drew together. "Lie? He's a doctor and has a business in California."

A business, not a practice. Meg glanced past the mayor's right arm. Someone moved in kitchen. She had seen part of a torso—a shoulder—near the table where she and Gilby drank coffee whenever they came to discuss the annual goals and budget of Sweet Creek's police department.

"How long have you known him, Hudson?" Before he could respond, she went on. "Carleton's *not* a medical doctor. I checked. He was a patient of a Sacramento cosmetology clinic."

Leland's jaw jumped. "That's private information you're digging up, Chief."

Disbelief shot through Meg. He wasn't questioning that Carleton had lied, but that she'd discovered the man was a fraud. "Are you not concerned he lied to *you,* Mayor?"

The man flapped a hand. "People lie all the time about things. It doesn't make them the bad guy."

Excuse me? In her experience most people were decent, law-abiding citizens. They did not lie and cheat *all the time.* But…could Leland be including himself as one of those all-the-time liars? Stepping into the shoes of mayor of Sweet Creek, he'd taken an oath that upheld integrity and rightfulness and sincerity. It meant having a clear conscience. Evidently Leland was hiding something.

"I'll ask again, Mr. Mayor…how well do you know Roland Carleton?"

"We're working out a business deal."

"Care to elaborate?"

His eyes narrowed. "Am I being investigated, Chief?"

Ethan's words less than a month ago.

Should you be? "No, but I am wondering why things start happening in my town shortly after a stranger comes around and claims he's something he's not."

Chuckling, Leland shook his head. "Let it go, Meg. Roland's okay. I give you my word. We're hunting buddies. That's it in a nutshell."

Except Carleton's hunting skills were less than stellar.

"Now," Leland continued, "what are we looking at for cleanup costs of that paint damage?"

"We won't know until Roy does an estimate." Roy Innis owned and managed Sweet Creek's only insurance business; the one Leland's Realty sold him fifteen years ago.

Leland nodded. "I'll talk to him in the morning. Are we done here, Chief?"

Not yet. "Do you know where Mr. Carleton is, Mayor?"

"Jeez, Meg, give it a rest. He's an okay guy, all right?" He moved to close the door. "I'll drop by to-morrow, see who we can round up as graffiti busters." And then she was facing wood.

Slowly, Meg walked back to her truck. Gut instinct didn't lie. She couldn't put her finger on it, but some-thing was off. Pulling from the curb she saw Leland's house, bold as brass, in her right side mirror. *Who* had been in his kitchen?

The question revolved in Meg's mind until she entered her home twenty minutes later and heard the washing machine stop. In the bathroom, the shower ran.

Beau had tossed in a load of laundry before break-fast? Incredible.

Setting her purse and keys on the table in the hallway, she headed for the laundry room. Might as well toss the clothes in the dryer while she made him breakfast.

Not clothes. One item. His navy-blue hoodie—with yellow paint on the left elbow....

Oh, son. You didn't.

Monday morning Beau drove his pickup to school with a knot in his gut. He'd barely gotten any sleep the night before, and breakfast this morning...forget it. He wanted to puke, the fear was so intense.

Man, was he in the friggin' toilet. So far down, he didn't think he'd ever see the light of day again.

He pictured the faces of his friends. Or *former* friends. Both Randy and Zena phoned last night and told him where to go in an anatomically impossible way.

"I thought you were my best friend," Randy had spat into Beau's ear.

Zena hadn't been quite so kind. She'd called Beau every universally vile name she could think of, then slammed down the receiver so hard the crash damn near busted his eardrum.

Worst was Miles. His *no*-call said a boatload more than either Randy's or Zena's rants.

The funny part was he hadn't ratted on any of them. Not one stinking name crossed his lips yesterday morning after he innocently walked into the kitchen and saw his mom with his hoodie laid out on the counter like a trophy carcass. God, had her eyes been daggers, he'd've been dead meat on the spot....

"What's this, Beau?" she'd asked, calm as a chill pill, her finger on the smudge of yellow paint.

"Nothin'." He had walked over to the loaf of bread by the toaster—as if his life wasn't about to turn inside out right that second.

"Guess where I've been this morning?" she asked, in that chilly way she had when she was ready to froth at the mouth.

He flipped two slices into the toaster. "How should I know? I was asleep till, like, fifteen minutes ago."

That set her off. It still stunned him how strong she was for a skinny woman. She'd spun him around like a top, pushed her face into his and told him about Gilby's call, about going into town, about the *destruction*—her word—he and his friends had left behind.

Well, he'd taken it until she stopped to catch a breath, then he'd snarled, "I wasn't there, okay?"

"Is that so?" As always her expression told him of her distrust.

"Yes, that's so!" That's when he pushed away from her. "Why can't you ever *believe* me?" He'd been so mad, his eyes stung. "I came home an hour before my curfew last night, Mom. Why do you suppose that was? Huh? Because things were happening I didn't like." He whirled around, vision blurred so much he barely saw the toaster. "I don't care that you don't believe me. *I* know what *I* did and it wasn't smearing graffiti on a bunch of stores."

"How did paint get on your jacket?"

Jeez, she was like bad dream, coming back again and again and again. "I don't wanna talk about it." He had no intention of telling her that Miles had called him a whiny wuss when Beau opted out of the game. When he'd watched the guy scrawl paint all over the window of the coffee shop that had given Beau his first real job. The shop where classmate Chandra Timms laughed and joked with the customers and sent him smiles so sweet he lost his tongue.

Behind him, his mom sighed. "If you don't talk about it, this situation will not better itself, Beau."

This situation had nothing to do with graffiti on walls and everything to do with their relationship. He blinked hard. If only she knew how much *he* wanted something better between them. She was his mother, the one who'd been there since day one.

The one who stuck up for him every time his dad dumped him like so much garbage.

Hunching his shoulders, he looked across the kitchen. "Mom, all I can tell you is I didn't do anything wrong."

The furnace kicked in as he forced himself to hold her gaze. Finally she nodded. "All right. If you say it's true, then it is."

He hadn't felt the tension in his shoulders until he

recognized the ache of relief. "Thanks," he said, and for an instant wanted to put his arms around her and hide in her neck the way he had as a kid when his emotions were thick enough to swallow.

Instead the toast popped and he'd gotten down to the business of spreading a fat layer of peanut butter across each slice.

Five minutes after Beau drove off for school in the morning mist, Meg swung her truck toward Ethan's place.

Might as well get this over with, she thought. Late yesterday afternoon she'd talked to Miles Ralston and Randy Leland, as well as their respective fathers, Jock and Linc. The men had not been impressed about the teenagers' machinations, which each boy admitted to after a half-dozen threats of punishment, the least of which was no wheels for a month.

Still, the investigation hadn't endeared the men to the law or to Meg.

"You'd best keep that rat kid of yours out of our sight for a while 'cuz he ain't welcome round here." Jock's words. Linc issued a similar oath.

Meg gripped the steering wheel. Jock Ralston would do well to stay out of *her* sight for a while. *Damn bully.* She knew why the man's son painted Ethan's initials on the window of the Hair Do. Over the summer months, Jock had no doubt stomped and cursed—*great role model for his son*—about Ethan's decision to close the rifle range thereby eliminating his position as manager.

From third grade on Jock had never liked Ethan. The details of how their animosity developed remained ambiguous. Perhaps it was because Jock's father, a redneck from the get-go, had poured his values onto his son, and when Jock had assumed Meg was *his* friend and she'd ignored him, he'd seen it as a personal insult.

Or maybe it was because she'd always had a soft spot for the underdog, which Jock was not. *Come on, Meg, own up. You loved Ethan the second you saw him.*

Ethan, with his dark, haunting eyes and gentle soul offered an assurance she missed within herself, some intrinsic power to reach higher, to defeat failure.

She would do well to follow in those footsteps, turn the tide of her insecurities. *And stop looking in the mirror and imagining the worst. Give yourself a chance.*

Give them both a chance.

God, how she wanted that.

Tatters of fog hung in the trees and shrouded his house and buildings. The lagoon was hidden behind a blanket of gray. Meg pulled up to park beside his truck and for a moment sat in the stillness. Dewdrops dampened branches and grass and his porch roof.

To the right, his studio door opened and he stepped onto its stoop, a tall figure at ease with his surroundings and enveloping mist. The rottweiler bounded past his legs to trot down the path as Meg climbed from her vehicle. Lifting a hand in acknowledgment, Ethan strode after the canine.

A burgundy flannel shirt draped his shoulders, then tapered into the brown belt securing the familiar Wranglers to his lean hips. In his hand he held a pencil, which he slipped into his shirt pocket. He'd been sketching. Meg wondered what time his day had begun.

"Had coffee yet?" he asked as he approached.

"If you've got a pot on, I'll have a cup, but don't go to any trouble."

"No trouble for you. I just brewed a batch." He

stopped in front of her, ran a finger down her cheek, then dipped his head and caught her lips in a good-morning kiss that closed her eyes. "Mmm. Much better than coffee," he said softly after it was done.

She had looked at his face a million times before, had drowned in its secrets, lost herself to the essence that was him and only him. And in that moment, looking once more, she knew.

She loved him.

And if she was honest, a part of her had never stopped loving him over the past nineteen years. Her marriage to Doug had masked the hole in her heart where she'd buried Ethan.

She opened her mouth to tell him, but he set a finger against her lips and smiled, and she wondered if he sensed what she was about to disclose. In their youth, he'd been sensitive to her thoughts, her feelings, to the point she believed they shared one spirit.

Entwining his fingers with hers, he started back to the studio. "Let's have that coffee first."

Before he *heard* words she might need to take back.

Because he didn't trust her to say them without reservation.

The notion depressed her. *Well, Meg. How can you expect him to trust you when you can't trust yourself?*

Touché.

On the studio steps, she halted and said what she'd come for, the police business. "Linc's and Jock's boys were involved in a graffiti spree in town. They signed your initials to the mess."

He grunted softly, shook his head.

"They'll be going to juvenile court," she added.

"Too bad. Beau?"

"Walked away."

And there it was, his smile again. "Let's get that coffee."

They entered the studio, Lila slipping in beside them to lie on a mat under a large drafting table. Ethan's worktable.

Meg wandered over. A dozen photos of her were scattered across the surface. The photos he'd shot the night of their canoe trip on Blue Lake. Meg stared in awe. Was that her, that woman whose elegant yet sultry silhouette stood etched against a golden moon?

"Like them?" Ethan asked, standing behind her shoulder.

Her throat hurt. "They're beautiful. I didn't know I looked…" *So ordinary, so regular.* "Ethan, I need to tell you something."

He turned her around, face-to-face, eye to eye. "I know."

"You do?" Her heart jumped. Had someone told him? Had Beau? Her brother, Ash?

"You've got a secret," he continued. "I've felt it in my heart for a while." He brushed aside a lock of hair that had fallen over her right brow. "Every time I touch you in certain places, honey, you dodge out of the way. It's not hard to figure out the reason. But it's all right."

Now or never. Get it over with—and move on. If he chose to walk away, she wouldn't stop him. She couldn't bear these seesawing emotions whenever she was with him. She wanted to make love to him as much as he wanted it. And if he loved her…*okay.*

If he didn't…

Then at least you'll know.

Meg swallowed hard. "Seven years ago they found a lump in my left breast. It was cancerous. I had a mas-

tectomy, then reconstructive surgery. There's scarring…
and things are different. And I won't be able to breast-
feed in a normal way should I have more kids, and if
these things are going to be issues for you, I need to
know now. I need to know if you're—"

He pulled her against him, hard, tight. "Shut up for
a minute." Kisses rained on her hair. "I am not going
anywhere. Ever. Get that straight right now. You're stuck
with me, lady. I'm never letting you go again."

Her chin wobbled. Oh, God, she was going to cry.
Cry and make a mess all over him. And yet she couldn't
stop her arms from sliding around his waist, couldn't
stop from burrowing into his chest.

Couldn't stop the tears. She hadn't cried in years. She
had mourned, grieved, suffered. But she hadn't cried.
Not since that first day, when she heard the diagnosis.

She clung like a child, fisting Ethan's shirt in her
hands. She cried for the lost years between them, the
silly fears she had harbored. She cried for her inability
to see beauty in herself the way Ethan had with those
photographs.

She cried for her failed marriage, for Beau despair-
ing over his father.

And she cried for Ethan.

Ethan, suffering narrow-mindedness in childhood
and bigotry as an adult. Ethan, enduring the worst in-
justice of all—prison—for something he didn't do.
Ethan, drowning his demons with alcohol.

Years of heartache poured through her tears.

He rocked her in his arms, murmured against her
hair. "That's it, baby. Let it all out. I'm here."

Yes, she thought, breathing the scent of him. He
was here.

At last her sobs altered into hiccups, then sniffles. Ethan kissed her forehead, reached for the tissue box on the drafting table.

"I must be a mess," she said, swiping at her eyes, cheeks, running a palm against her nose.

"Nah. You needed a good cry, is all."

She released a half laugh. "Yeah, guess I did."

"Still want a coffee?"

"I'd love one." She followed him across the room to a scratched dining room hutch housing myriad albums instead of chinaware and a coffee maker. He poured a cup, splashed in a spoonful of cream—exactly how she liked her java.

He nodded to the back door. "Let's go outside for a bit. Nothing like fresh air to clear the sinuses."

God, he'd always understood her need to collect herself. Mugs in hand, they stood on the small wooden stoop. Under a stronger sun the fog abated, leaving misty rags clinging to the near-leafless trees climbing the hill.

Ethan said, "Every morning I wake up in awe that my grandfather left this property to me."

The indomitable Davis O'Conner, who had not wanted to understand or know his grandson. O'Conner, Meg knew, had been against his daughter's marriage to Jackson Red Wolf.

"Old Davis didn't care much about the land," Ethan went on, "but neither did he want it going to anyone else after he died."

"I think he loved you in his own skewed way."

Ethan snorted softly. "I can count on one hand the number of times we had a conversation. Every few years he'd get a guilt complex, phone Mom and she'd haul me out here. The last time was when he was dying and refused to go to the hospital." He looked at Meg. "Know what he said?"

She shook her head, mesmerized by the depth of pain in his eyes.

"Since I was part Blackfoot I'd have a *feel* for the environment." Ethan snorted softly. "Like I was some kind of noble oddity. My own grandfather."

"You are, you know."

"What, a noble oddity?"

"Noble."

A corner of his mouth twitched. "Now *you're* biased."

"Maybe. Probably." Her eyes clung to his. "I love you, Ethan."

And there they were. Three words. Out there, floating in the mist, settling like dewdrops on his shinning hair, his big shoulders, in his dark, dark eyes.

She watched him swallow. "*Meggie.* I never thought I'd…hear you say it again."

Courage in her heart. "I want to make love with you. If…if you still want to."

Cupping his free hand around her nape, he set his forehead to hers. "Lady, you don't know how much I want to. I've wanted it since I was eighteen. Hell, since I was sixteen."

"Then," she whispered, "let's set a date."

"Tonight?"

She chuckled. "Anxious?"

"Aren't you?"

"What do you think?" She kissed his mouth. "Beau's spending next weekend on the ranch with Ash and Rachel."

"Jeez, woman. You're keeping me hard all week?"

Meg canted him a look. "We can have nightly phone calls."

He groaned. "You do want to kill me."

"No," she said, gazing into her coffee, suddenly shy. "I want our time to be perfect."

"It will, honey. Look at me." He lifted her chin, then took her hand and laid it over his heart. "You've been here all my life. Me seeing your scars, you seeing mine, is not going to change that."

Lord, if she wasn't careful she'd be blubbering all over him again. "Thank you."

"You're welcome." A slanted grin.

Laughing at their formality, Meg set her mug on the bench beside the door. "Well then. Till next weekend."

"Till tonight," he countered. "And Megs? Call when you're under the covers in bed."

A quiver ran between her pelvic bones. Forget tonight. If work weren't waiting, Meg would have him this instant. With a giddy smile, she headed around the building for her truck. She had its door open when Helen's blue pickup sped into the yard.

"I'm glad I caught you together," the older woman said, stepping from the Ford's cab. Her eyes switched from Meg to Ethan. "There's something I need to tell you."

Chapter Thirteen

"What is it, Mom?" Ethan asked when his mother's worried gaze clung to his. "What's happened?" A chill tripped across his scalp. Although his mother didn't own the latest fashions, her clothes were always tidy on her body, her makeup fresh and her hair brushed into a ponytail or knot on her head. Today her blouse hung untucked at the back and her hair straggled from half-protruding pins—as though she had walked here in a windstorm.

But what bothered him more than her harried appearance was the way she chewed her cheek. The habit was old as Ethan and spoke of the depth of her apprehension.

He took her arm. "Why don't we go into the house? I'll make us a pot of rose hip tea." His mother's favorite drink.

"All right." Without hesitation, she went up the porch steps.

Over his mother's head, Ethan caught Meggie's gaze. *I'm glad you're here,* he wanted to tell her. He had no idea what trouble his mom might be in; what he did know was he'd never seen her *this* distraught, and having Meggie present eased some of his trepidation.

In the kitchen he set the kettle to boil.

Squeezing her fingers, his mother walked back and forth. "I should have told you long ago, son. I shouldn't have kept it a secret."

Ethan went to where Meggie leaned against the counter, her gun belt glossy in the October sunshine sweeping the patio glass. His foot rested against hers. She'd set her hands back on the counter and he did the same, linking their pinky fingers between them.

"What secret?" he asked calmly while his heart jackhammered.

"About Hudson and me."

"The mayor?" Ethan raised his eyebrows.

"Yes. Oh, son." His mother stopped her pacing; her arms hugged her chest as she looked at Ethan. "I…I had an affair with him."

Three beats of silence. Long enough for Meggie's hand to curl around his palm in support. He said, "When?"

"Just before…your father died."

Ethan's heart rate leveled. "Mom, that was thirty years ago."

Clearly in a trance of worry, she paced again. "I was so lonely, so heartbroken over your daddy's injuries. Deep in my heart I knew he'd never be the same again. And then he… He was a wonderful man, such a gentle soul and I loved him beyond words. I'd taken a part-time bookkeeping job in Hudson's real estate office on Saturday mornings."

And Hudson Leland, a married man back then, took advantage of a young woman's sorrow, the wife of a comatose Blackfoot man. Ethan wanted to box someone's ears, preferably those of Hudson Leland. As if sensing his agitation, Meggie's fingers tightened.

His mother pushed at a loose strand of hair. "Your daddy and I... We weren't looking for riches. All we wanted was to live a decent life, raise our little family. But when he died, I quit teaching and put all our savings into the shop he'd started. I couldn't bear the thought of closing the store, of selling off his dreams."

She looked across the room at Ethan. "I wanted to keep his legacy for you. Not in things, but through the symbols and crafts of his heritage."

And Ethan had shunned that heritage. "Mom, I'm sorry."

She shook her head. "It's not your fault, it was never your fault. It was me. I should have understood better what you were going through as a child and a teenager with those...boys."

He offered a small smile. "I survived."

"Yes," she said. "You have, and beautifully." Her gaze settled on the woman beside Ethan. "That's why I wanted you both to know about this sordidness, and its repercussions all these years later. I'm so, so ashamed." She shook her head. "But if you two are to have a chance together, you need to know everything."

Ethan pushed off the counter. "What repercussions?"

"When you were young, and Linc Leland and Jock Ralston gave you so much grief at school, I went to the principal and informed him of what was going on." She held up a hand when Ethan swore. "I know what you're thinking. Had I left well enough alone, maybe things would've died down, run their own course. But then, Hudson visited me at the shop one day, said that if *I* didn't back off from his son, he'd expose our affair in a way that would put the onus on me." Her mouth crimped. "I was afraid. I didn't want my father involved. I don't know what he might have done had he known about the whole sleazy mess."

Ethan could imagine what Davis O'Conner might have done. Taken a gun on a visit to Hudson Leland.

"So rather than go to the law, I let you put up with Linc." Tears welled. "Oh, God. I'm so, so sorry, Ethan, so ashamed."

He went over, gave her a hug. "It's history, Ma. I've long since stopped fretting about Linc." Not that he ever had. But she needed to hear the words for her own reassurance.

"There's more. Last week, Hudson made the same threat if I didn't convince you to stop building the helping-horse stable and reinstate the rifle range."

In his peripheral vision, Ethan saw Meggie step toward him, felt her hand curl around his forearm. He forced himself to keep his fingers loose at his sides. She said, "On my way back to the office, I'll pop over and pay the mayor a visit."

"I'm coming with you," he stated.

"No." Her eyes were blue ice. "Ethan, let me do this alone."

"I take care of my own, Meggie."

"I know you do, but this is not the time to play hero. If Leland's threatened one of my citizens, then it becomes my domain."

"I'll see you there, then." He paced to the front door, flung it open. Lila raced outside to his pickup, eager for a ride. "Mom," he called over his shoulder, "go home."

"Ethan—" She hurried onto the porch after him. "Meg…I don't want to cause trouble. Please. Maybe… maybe Hudson was joking."

Barking an unpleasant laugh, Ethan spun around. "Mom, the guy is intimidating you." Ethan wanted to smash his face. "We'll see what he has to say to me, someone his own size."

Meggie held up an index finger as a gesture for him to calm down, which ticked him off even more. This was his fight, his mother.

"Helen, what the mayor has done is a form of extortion, and that's against the law. If it makes you feel easier I'll have a chat with him, see what he has to say."

"I don't want trouble," she repeated.

"It'll be okay." Meggie rubbed his mom's shoulder, then followed him down the porch stairs. "Ethan, you're too angry. Let me handle this."

He shot a look back. His mother stood on the threshold, shoulders drooping, eyes anxious, and he realized with a stab to his heart that she was getting on in years. It fueled his determination to punch Hudson Leland in the mouth.

"Meggie," he said, dragging his gaze back to the woman who had wept on his shirt not thirty minutes ago. "I won't have anyone bully my family." Time to end it here and now.

"All right." She set her small hand on his chest where his heart pounded like a warrior's song. "We'll go together, but promise you'll let me do the talking." Her eyes locked on his for several beats.

"Fine."

"And you won't start a fight verbally or otherwise? Because I'll toss you in jail to cool your heels, Ethan, if it comes to that."

"You have my word. And just so *you* know, I'm in-stating myself as my mother's advisor." His gaze flicked to the older woman. "However, you and I are going to talk about this when we're done with Leland."

He saw she understood. He didn't like her job. He didn't like that she dealt with the jackasses of the world. He didn't like that she put herself in danger. Most of all, cop or not, he didn't like her fighting *his* battles. He never had.

"We'll talk," she said. "Let's take my truck. Helen, you okay to go back to your place?"

"I wish I'd never opened my mouth." Hands clenched together, his mother remained rooted on the porch.

Ethan went around to the Silverado's passenger side, paused before opening the door. "Mom, it'll be okay. *I'm* okay." He offered a truce grin across the truck's hood at the woman he loved. "Megs will keep me lev-elheaded. She always did." And that was the truth.

He told Lila to stay on guard then climbed into the truck cab as Meggie turned the ignition. He waited until she wheeled out of his yard and started up the lane to the Lake Road.

He said, "You know I'm crazy about you."

"I know."

"I don't want you hurt."

"I know that, too. However, don't interfere in my work again." She shot him a look. "Investigations are what I do for a living, Ethan."

They rode in silence for a half mile while he digested

her command—and it was a command no matter how he looked at it. Could he blame her? If they were to have a future together, he'd damned well have to get used to her take-charge methods when it came to unsavory behaviors in the town she was hired to protect.

"You gonna stay mad at me?" he asked, not liking the strain between them.

Her brows hiked. "Who said I'm mad?"

"Huh. Could've fooled me." Disgruntled that she'd misread his meaning—that he wanted to be *her* protector—he focused on the road canopied by dark branches.

In his peripheral vision he saw her push a hand through the thick cap of her hair. "Look," she said. "Sometimes police work is hard even for family members to grasp. But since we've got a few minutes before town, let's discuss it now. Being female *and* without a breast does not make me weak or helpless or unable to accomplish my job to the utmost of my ability. I've been chief of police for six years and not once, *not once,* have I had to rely on Gilby or Sally or Pearl or anyone else to do the job for me. Nor have I hidden behind my desk and sent Gilby to do the dirty work."

That she'd see his concern as a link to her former disease spiked his ire. "You about done?"

"Not yet." She glanced over. "I understand your anger because of your mother. Really, I do. I also understand your wanting to keep me safe. We've barely found each other again, and you want to be my guardian angel and, believe me, Ethan, I want you beside me every step we take into the future. But you cannot be my shield. Most of all, you cannot assume I don't know what I'm doing."

"I never said you didn't know what you were doing."

"Maybe not in so many words, but your actions leave me wondering."

"About what?" He was still dealing with "weak and helpless."

"If my work will come between us."

"It won't." She had it all wrong. He was a rescuer at heart—of the land, of eagles, of barred owls. And now Meggie was part of the package. No, she was the *main* package. He'd die before allowing something or someone to hurt her—breast or no breast.

"Ethan?"

"Your former disease has nothing to do with how I feel, Meggie. *You* understand *that*."

He recognized the lift of tension when her knuckles gained a modicum of color on the steering wheel.

"All right."

"Just stay out of the line of fire," he muttered.

"As you've seen, I'm good at dodging bullets. I plan to keep it that way."

Somehow her *plan* did nothing to set him at ease.

"What a god-awful mess."

Every time Meg saw the yellow swirls of graffiti along Cardinal Avenue, she said a grateful prayer Beau had refused to play by Miles Ralston's rules. "I'll be asking the juvie judge for a few hundred hours of community service."

"Think it'll happen? We're talking Hudson Leland's grandson."

She knew he was remembering his own episode with a Wyoming judge. "I'll *make* it happen. If I have to yank every string to do it." She pulled into an angled slot outside the town office, a white Victorian building once the home of the town's founder. "Let me see if he's in. Sometimes he doesn't work before ten."

"Lazy ass to boot. Don't know how he got the votes."

"If you recall, no one else wanted the job."

"They were too afraid to run against him."

"That, too." Not caring a whit if they were seen, she leaned across the console and gave him a quick kiss. "Be right back."

"Whoa," he said, catching her waist before she could climb out of the cab. "What kind of kiss was that?"

"Eth—"

He laid his mouth on hers, waltzed his tongue around until each cell in her body sang a high-pitched refrain. When he was done, he set her back in the seat, dazed.

"We had our first tiff," he said. "We needed to clear the air."

"Clear the air?" Laughing, she finger combed her hair. "You've addled my brain."

"That's good. I want you thinking of me."

"I never stop thinking about you." Her eyes hooked on his. *Even in my dreams you're there.*

"Let's get out of here before you need to arrest me for doing something hot and hard in front of the town office." Opening the door, he stepped from the truck.

She was outside in a flash. "Where are you going?"

"To talk to Leland. Can't have you going in half-dizzy."

"Very sneaky, Mr. Red Wolf." But she couldn't stop the grin as she rounded the vehicle. "I am holding you to your promise, however. No interfering."

He offered a Scout's honor.

Satisfied, she led him into the building. Leland was in, as was his secretary. "Beryl, I need to speak with the mayor a moment. Won't take long," Meg added when

Beryl cast a furtive look toward the closed door with its Mayor Hudson Leland in gold lettering at eye level. "Five minutes, tops."

"What about…him?" Beryl hiked her chin at Ethan leafing through a magazine.

Meg hauled in her disgust. *Damn it.* What was the matter with this town? But she knew. Not the town. Beryl was Jock Ralston's wife, and Jock had never been Ethan's buddy, and certainly not since he'd shut down the rifle range.

To hell with it.

"Mr. Red Wolf will join my discussion with the mayor."

Ethan hid his surprise well. Tossing down the magazine, he walked over to Meg. "Trying to make a point?" he whispered when Beryl went down the corridor to knock on the mayor's door.

"Damn straight," she muttered.

"Which is…?"

"I've never been partial to jackasses or slimeballs."

His smile was slow and curled through her belly with the headiness of a heated Grand Marnier shooter.

Beryl returned, high heels click-clacking on the hardwood. "Mayor Leland will see you now."

"Thank you, Beryl. I owe you."

"Yes," the woman said promptly. "You do. Mr. Leland is a very busy man."

Meg rolled her eyes and headed down the hallway to the mayor's spacious corner office.

"Hey, Meg. Ethan." The man said magnanimously, gesturing to the four leather chairs fanning his desk in a half circle. "How can I help you two?"

Meg chose to stand, as did Ethan. She said, "Hudson, I've come on behalf of a complaint that concerns you."

His eyes widened. "On what premise?"

"Possible extortion."

Leather squawked as he sat back and gripped the arms like a man ready to jump off a springboard. "That's a helluva charge, Chief."

"It's not a charge, Mayor." *Yet.* "It concerns the complaint issued by a Sweet Creek citizen, Mrs. Helen Red Wolf. She claims you threatened to expose her affair with you some thirty years ago if she did not convince her son, Mr. Ethan Red Wolf—" Meg gestured to the man standing several feet away "—to reinstate the rifle range on his property. That's blackmail, Mayor."

"I never said any such thing to Helen. She's lying if she told you that." He puffed out his chest. "There's no proof I did anything wrong. It's her word against mine."

"So, you didn't mention your affair with her?" Meg persisted.

"No."

"And you didn't speak to her at all on the Saturday of the Harvest Moon craft fair?"

His gaze darted to Ethan. "Not that I remember."

Meg's gut said the man was lying.

"But there was an affair, right?"

"No!" Sweat poked from his skin. "Look, it happened once. That's not an affair."

"Then what was it? A one-night stand? A fling?"

"Neither. She was lonely, I was lonely. It happened. End of story. I did not threaten her about it."

"You didn't hold that *one time* over her head when your son harassed Mr. Red Wolf in high school? When she requested that the principal intervene?"

Leland rose, planted his hands on his desk. "What crud is she feeding you?"

Meg felt Ethan's anger. She lifted a hand in front of his chest as though to hold him in place. "Mr. Leland," she continued mildly. "Threats or coercion with the intent to force someone to do something against their will, or cause public exposure, is illegal. Let this be a warning, all right? For your sake and mine, and the Red Wolfs."

"Don't forget who you work for, Meg."

"Strike two," Ethan said softly.

"Is that another threat, Mayor?" Meg asked.

"Not at all." The man flashed a glare at Ethan. "And I wasn't talking to you."

"Ditto. Have a nice day, Mayor." Quietly stepping back, he turned on a heel and exited the office.

"Meg," Leland called as she proceeded to leave as well. "I don't want this in the weekend report."

"It's a warning, Mayor. Not a charge."

"Good. And that graffiti?" He waved a dismissive hand. "Just a bunch of kids being silly."

Of course it was. The graffiti concerned his grandson.

"We'll see how silly the judge considers it."

Leland glared across his polished desk. "You're making a mistake, Meg. Just like you did with Roland Carleton who, by the way, *is* a doctor—a psychologist—looking to buy property here, maybe set up an office here. He could be an asset for your *friend* and his—" he scowled "—riding venture."

She held in her surprise. "Why didn't you tell me earlier?" When she'd grilled the man outside Leland's house.

A shrug. "What a guy does for a living isn't my business."

"Oh? Is this one of those mayoral blind-eye moments?" His smile wasn't kind. "Be careful, Meg."

"Right." She turned to go.

"What do you see in Red Wolf, anyway?"

Slowly she turned. *Please be out of the building, Ethan. Please don't hear this.* "Would this concern the office of the mayor?"

"If there's a conflict of interest."

"How so?"

"Favors."

"I'll pretend I didn't hear that." She strode from his office, down the hallway and out of the building—to Ethan, arms crossed, leaning against the driver's door of her truck. Ethan, with his tousled hair, cappuccino skin and brown, brown eyes.

What do you see in Red Wolf?

A man, she thought. *A fine and honest man.*

"Ready to go?" she asked.

He pushed away to open the door for her. "I'll walk to Mom's. By the way, Linc Leland went in a minute ago. Bet the old man's itching to give him an earful."

Meg climbed behind the wheel, rolled down the window. "Linc gets an update every Monday and Friday."

"Why? He's not on the town council."

"Because he's the mayor's son and the mayor's bidder."

"That's breaking confidence."

A short, humorless laugh escaped. "And that's new in politics?"

His expression was solemn. "How do you put up with it, Meggie? How do you put up with that kind of browbeating?"

He'd heard Leland's question, after all. Something prickled her skin and stung her heart. She knew why he asked. *This isn't your battle, Ethan.* "In what way?" she asked calmly.

"Him soliciting personal questions, trying to make you second-guess yourself as a cop."

"As long as he doesn't interfere with my duties, the mayor can say whatever he wishes. My investigations will prove my integrity." She turned the ignition. "Talk to you later, then?"

"You're avoiding the issue."

"Not at all. I'm asking you—again—not to get between me and my job."

He stepped away from the truck as if she'd smacked him. "Keep safe," he said, before striding down the sidewalk.

"Ethan—" *Damn it.* How had she not realized the impact her work would have on him? Police people dealt with the underbelly of society, which often meant they endured name-calling, spitting, bruises—all to deflate and deflect arguments and fights and anger—at a cost to their own emotions, their own respect. And sometimes that underbelly had "Mayor" bolted on its door.

She watched him walk away. *Please understand,* she thought bleakly.

Trouble was he understood too well.

About to set the vehicle in Reverse, she paused when her eyes caught the word Michelin on the tire of the SUV beside her Silverado, Linc's SUV. Latitude X-Ice tires. She got of her truck and crouched between the two vehicles to inspect the tread of the left-rear tire. With a pen from her shirt pocket, she picked at mud and dirt, leaves and stones until the tread was clean. Nothing. Not a nick to be seen. She'd have to ask Linc to move the vehicle a couple feet.

She stood and eyed the door of the town offices. He would be in his father's office wanting to know why Ethan Red Wolf had waited outside beside Meg McKee's truck.

With a long sigh, she went up the steps and back inside the old Victorian building.

Chapter Fourteen

Home bell rang and Beau grabbed his knapsack off the back of his desk chair to crowd with the rest of the kids through the classroom door. Like always at this time of day, the hallways overflowed. Kids hollering at each other, lockers clanging, body odor rank. He'd never admit it, but in another year he'd miss these final moments of the school day. There was a mood about home time, he sensed, which he would not experience again anywhere, or at any other time in his life.

Outside kids hung around in groups, yakking and laughing and strolling toward the seven buses lined along the sidewalk. Beau headed for the parking lot and his pickup.

Three girls threw him sour looks. All day the glances had been hard to swallow, but slowly his skin tough-ened. Still, it irked him people thought he'd tattled on his friends because, *damn it,* he hadn't.

Approaching his pickup, he noticed his cousin Daisy—and Chandra Timms from the coffee shop—leave a group of popular girls and walk toward him.

"Hey, cuz," Daisy greeted. "Miles and Randy are over there." She nodded toward the back of the parking lot, "They want to talk to you."

His heartbeat sped up. "Figures." He darted a look at Chandra. Her eyes brimmed concern.

I can take care of myself, he wanted to say.

"Well, just so you know," Daisy said, "they've been spreading junk about you spraying the town then telling Aunt Meggie it was them." She sent his former friends a hard look. "They're lying. I know that and Chandra knows that and so does everyone else, but if you don't do something soon, or speak up, they're going to believe *them.*"

"I agree," Chandra chimed in.

He wanted nothing more than to take her hand and hold on.

"Thanks," he managed. A crowd was gathering where Miles and Randy stood with their girlfriends and some other kids he had once called friends.

"Hey, rattail," Miles called. "Hiding behind girls now?"

Snickers and giggles. At least it wasn't gut-busting laughter, and Beau noticed some of the kids were looking at the ground like they didn't want to meet his eyes. A tiny ray of hope sparked in him. Not all the kids voted with Miles and Randy.

Daisy and Chandra at his side, he walked toward the group.

His cousin whispered, "A lot don't believe them. They're just scared of Miles."

Because Miles was four months short of nineteen, pushed back into school by a father who wanted his son to achieve West Point grades, not dropout status—a path Beau was destined to tour if he didn't pull up *his* socks, as his mom loved to point out.

Suddenly Beau no longer wanted to travel that route. With Chandra's respect and Daisy's support, he squared his shoulders. He'd always been at the top of his class; he could be again.

He stopped five feet away. At six-two, his eyes were level with Miles. "Heard you're slinging lies about me."

"Not lies, punk. Truth." Miles flicked a look at Randy. Zena and her friends giggled beside Beau's ex-buddy. "We all know you did that paint job. We were there."

"Funny, that's not what I remember."

"Yeah?" Miles sneered, amusement gone. He stepped closer. "We say you did it. Don't we, guys?"

No one answered. Beau glanced at Zena; she avoided his gaze. She knew damned well he wasn't guilty. While Miles and Randy and their girls had been painting, he'd been sitting on a bench copping halfhearted feels from Zena. Until he got tired of her whining that he really didn't want to do "it" and Randy had laughed and drizzled his arm with paint. Disgusted with all of them, Beau had gotten into his truck and driven home.

"Don't we?" Miles snapped, eyes cold.

"It's like Miles says," Randy muttered, steering clear of Beau. "Even ratted to his *mom-my,*" he singsonged. "The police chief."

Some kids giggled.

Beau stared at his former best friend. "Right. I'm going to tell my mother I painted the town. Makes a ton of sense, Randy."

"Shut up." Miles gave Beau's shoulder a shove. "He meant you ratted on *us.*"

"No, *you* shut up." Beau shoved back, hard enough that Miles lost a step. "Here's an intellectual brain fart for *you.* She knew who I was with that night because she *asked* where I was going and *who* with. Like she does all the time." He glared around. "Like your parents do, Rennie, and yours, Zena, and yours, Randy. Y'all have curfews, just like me." He thumbed his chest. "And I've heard every one of you phone your mom to ask for more time, and *tell her* where you're at and who you're with." His eyes narrowed on Miles. "My mom already knew. I didn't have to tell her." He grabbed Chandra's hand. "Come on, let's get out of here."

"Just a sec." Miles blocked their path. "So she knew. You still blamed us."

Beau fisted his free hand. "I didn't have to, Ralston. You did that all on your own when you pointed fingers. See, my *friends*—" he shot Randy a look "—know I'd never rat on them. But they *do* know *you* would."

"Says who?"

"Says everyone who's been blamed for something you did, starting with setting that trash fire in the science lab two years ago." Beau glowered at a boy standing behind Randy. "Isn't that right, Pete?" Again he glared at Ralston. "And when you busted the principal's windshield with a rock and blamed Keith." The boy in question ducked from sight. "Yeah, like I'd take your word on anything, Ralston."

Whipping around, Beau started for his truck.

"Hey, I'm not done with you," Ralston yelled.

Beau ignored him. "You girls want a ride home?" he asked Chandra and his cousin.

"You bet," they chorused.

"Great." For the first time in two days, his heart held relief.

As promised in his studio that morning, Meg called Ethan at 11:00 p.m. God, had it been just this morning when she'd cried on his shirt? Exhausted from a long day, she lay curled on her side in her four-poster bed, staring into obscurity. He answered on the first ring.

"Hey," she said. "Still ticked with me?"

"I could never be ticked with you, Meggie."

Just disappointed. "At least, not for long, right?"

"Maybe two minutes." His smile traveled the line. "Are you in bed?" he asked.

"Yes, you?"

"Just got in."

A few beats passed and she pictured him, pillows propped against wood, an arm under his head. She wondered about the mattress size; likely, he would've bought a king to accommodate his six-three frame. She wondered whether he lay skin to sheets or whether he wore boxer shorts or pajama pants.

"What've you got on?" he asked, and a flush of heat permeated her belly. He might as well have looked inside her head.

"T-shirt."

Pause. "No panties?"

"It's an oversize T-shirt."

He blew a long sigh, and she could almost feel his breath fan her flesh. "Will you do something for me, baby?"

"Anyth—" She cleared her throat. "Anything."

"Touch your breasts."

"Ethan."

"Touch them, Meggie. And imagine my hands."

"I can't."

"Yes, you can. Touch them for me. Are you touching them?"

"I...all right, I'll try." Slowly she rolled onto her back, moved her left hand under the covers, drew up the T-shirt.

"Are you there, yet?"

Her fingers slid along her belly, tripped across her navel, stopped under the curve of her right breast. "I'm there," she said, her voice sounding oddly smoky in her ears.

"Which one?" he asked softly.

Bad or good. "The...normal one."

"They're *both* normal, sweetheart. Bring your hand up between them, spread your fingers and rub back and forth. Slowly. Very slowly. Close your eyes, focus on feeling. Feel what I'm feeling."

"What's that?" she whispered, glad for the night.

"You. *All* of you. You've lived in my heart for a thousand years, Meggie. Are you touching yourself?"

She imagined his long, brown fingers, strong, yet tender on her soft paleness. "Yes." Her flesh, her nipple, so sensitized.

"Are you hot?"

"Unbearably. I wish you were here, under the covers. I wish you were on me. *In me.* I wish...oh, Ethan, I wish so much."

Through her own trance, she heard his rapid breathing. "I'll be there soon, babe."

"I want you here tonight."

He chuckled. "Wouldn't look good to Beau, for one

thing. Second—" a sigh "—I need to get up at four to catch a flight to Seattle."

Her eyes opened. Her fingers stilled. And that quickly their moment vanished. He hadn't told her about his upcoming trip. She rolled again to her side. "For your paintings?"

"The gallery hosting my November show wants to go over some of projects. They phoned this afternoon."

"How long will you be gone?"

"Depending on whether I'm able to get all the supplies I need, I'm hoping to be out of there Thursday."

And suddenly she saw him in the city, dressed in tailored slacks, pressed shirt and tie, Laredo shoes polished, his hair lustrous and slicked back. He would be impressive, a businessman with distinct goals, assertive ambitions. He'd speak with industry people and the elite who could afford his work.

"Wish you could come along." Low and enigmatic, his voice slid into her musing.

She released a small sigh. "Me, too."

"Then why don't you? Let Gilby manage a couple days."

"Can't. I have commitments and investigations to wrap up."

She wanted to tell him about Linc owning the nicked tire, that she'd questioned him about pheasant hunting on private land. How he'd laughed and vowed to watch for No Trespassing signs *next* time.

She wanted to blurt her suspicions concerning Linc and Jock and Helen's break-in and the wounded eagle, the bird that had brought her and Ethan together and was healing to one day fly again.

But she kept the information to herself; she could

not breach the code of confidentiality, even for the man she loved.

"Gilby can't do the investigations?" he asked after a pause.

"No," she said firmly. "I won't hand over my files. We've already gone over this."

Seconds elongated and she sensed him pulling away, mentally, emotionally, slipping from the soft, warm sensuality they'd shared minutes before. In its place, pressed the coolness she feared. "Ethan?"

"When was the last time you took a holiday, Meggie? I'm not talking Labor Day weekend or Thanksgiving or Christmas. A real holiday, two weeks in the sun for fun."

"What's that got to do with going to Seattle?"

"Everything. If you came along I'd take an extra ten days, fly us to Puerto Vallarta or over to Hawaii. Drink margaritas in a cabana on some beach. Slather on the SPF 45. Dip our toes in water the color of your eyes."

The color of her eyes. His description sent a pang through her heart. He was a man with a depth of mystery that would take her ten lifetimes to unravel. God, he tempted her. But that would mean sharing a room with him, a bed, him seeing her naked—

Her heart pounded. *Don't shrink back again, Meg. You love him. You know he loves you.* Although he hadn't said the words, deep down she knew. She bit her tongue from saying *Yes!* and cursed her ingrained fears.

Resolutely she said, "I can't. Ask me any other time." She wanted to cry because he wouldn't ask again, wouldn't chase—as he hadn't when she walked away nineteen years ago. "You're making me choose," she said, poking herself mentally.

Silence. "Maybe I am. We're important, Megs. You and me." He paused. "Or did I read you wrong this morning?"

When she'd told him she loved him. "No. It's that things…"

"I know what I want," he said. "But maybe you don't. Not really. Maybe this will never be *your* time."

"Is that what you believe?"

He sighed and the sound hurt her heart. "I don't know what to believe anymore. This morning I thought different. This morning I thought we were going someplace."

"Ethan…"

"I'll see you when I get back. We'll talk then."

"Please understand."

"Honey, I understand more than you think."

"My job—"

"Comes first, I know."

It wasn't anger but disappointment that he would bring it back to that. She wanted to tell him she was afraid. Still afraid of intimacy with him—even though their relationship had progressed to take that next step— and that the fear was her problem not his.

"See you then," she whispered.

"'Night, Meggie." The phone clicked, the dial tone hummed in her ear. She was alone. Again.

He returned Friday, a day later than planned, and by the time he lugged his suitcase and a sack of groceries into the house, the sun had slunk behind Blue Mountain. Lila wriggled, tail to nose, in enthusiastic welcome.

"Settle down, old gal," he said, nearly stumbling over the dog in the entryway. "You'll tire of me quick enough and be looking for Mama Helen to take care of you again."

The animal let out a disagreeing woof. Ethan laughed softly and put an arm about the canine's neck. "Okay. I missed you, too. Think *she* missed me?"

Another woof.

"Yeah, you know who I mean. Of course she missed me."

He hadn't been able to stop thinking of the pain and horror she must have endured during her breast cancer days. And, God almighty, he wished he'd been there with her, for her, eased her fears. *You still can be...just don't act like a jerk when she doesn't agree with you on some things.*

Like her job.

In the kitchen he dumped his goods onto the counter, then headed for the laundry room to unload his travel-wrinkled clothes, toss them into the washing machine. A quick half cup of soap and the lid banged down.

"I'm hungry," he told the dog. "How about you?"

Three minutes later he stood at the sink cutting broccoli and carrots into a colander when Lila, her chest rumbling, rushed from her patio mat and through the house to the front door.

Drying his hands on a towel, Ethan went to answer the knock. Meggie stood under the porch light, a foil-wrapped glass dish in her hands. He drank her in: her shining hair; her blue, blue eyes; the pink sweater under a suede jacket. *Goddess,* he thought taking in the black skirt, the tall black boots that added three inches to her height. Goddess of his heart.

"Hey." His voice cracked. Jeez, he was fifteen again.

"I called earlier," she said. "But you weren't home, so I came by.... I wasn't sure if you'd eaten, or...or would be here."

But she'd taken the chance. "Just got in thirty minutes ago. Haven't checked the messages yet."

"I didn't leave one. I thought maybe you weren't taking my calls because of the way—"

He reached for her elbow. "Get in here and stop thinking nonsense." When he had her inside with the door closed, he cupped her face, and with the warm dish between them, kissed her long and deep. "Christ, I missed you," he muttered when it was done.

Her eyes glimmered. "Ethan, I'm sorry."

Setting his thumb to her mouth, he shook his head. "What's between us doesn't need apologies. I was an ass." He lifted a corner of the foil, sniffed. "Lasagna?"

"I was making a few batches to freeze. Beau loves lasagna."

"One of my favorites, too." He took the dish, headed for the kitchen. "Perfect with a spinach salad." He'd picked up a ready-made bag during his grocery stop. "Beau at the ranch?"

"Yes." She surveyed the sink with its vegetables. "I should've realized you were making supper."

Ethan set her homemade treat on the counter. "Meggie." Hoping to erase the worry in her eyes he said softly, "The spinach is in the fridge. Want to get it while I set the table?"

Through a light laugh she said, "Obvious I'm nervous, huh?"

His lips quirked. "A tad."

Over the next few minutes they prepared two salads, including a fruit mixture of grapes, orange wedges and cheese. When they sat to eat at his tiny table, he told her of his Seattle trip, of the paintings and sketches the gallery owner wanted to display in November, and she told him of the stolen pickup she recovered, the domestic fight between Silas Kent and his wife, Ruth, that she and Gilby were called to at one o'clock Wednesday morning. Gilby had taken Ruth to the hospital in Bozeman.

"Silas always was a mean bastard," Ethan commented. "Don't know why Ruth's stayed with him." The couple had gone to school with their mothers.

"Fear has tenacious roots sometimes," Meggie said, pushing a grape around on her plate.

Something told Ethan she spoke of herself rather than the troubled couple. He knew she was sensitive about her body, in particular her breasts. And about words from a man she had trusted, a man like Sutcliffe. Ethan shoved the thought aside, lest he do damage to a wall, and concentrated on the phone sex the night before he'd left for Seattle. Initially, she'd been reluctant— until he had encouraged her response.

Tonight, he thought. Tonight he would take it to the next level, one slow gentle step at a time.

He wanted to make love with her. He wanted her to love herself. To see she was a beautiful woman. A desirable woman.

Looking across the table, he felt his groin grow heavy, and suddenly he could stand the waiting no longer. Reaching, he caught her wrist. "You done eating?" She hadn't taken a bite for several minutes; hell, she'd barely eaten at all.

Her gaze scanned his half-empty plate. "Are you?"

"The only hunger I have here, Meggie, is for you.

I've had it for so damned long I can't remember when it started."

In the candlelight her eyes were blue seas. Linking her fingers with his she said, "Then let's get it done."

"You make it sound like a burden."

"I'm afraid."

A fierce ache ran through his heart. "Honey, this is me. We'll go as fast or slow as you want. I won't look where you don't want me to look, even though I want to see *all* of you." His fingers tightened on hers as he stood. "But enough talking. It's time." To Lila he said, "Mat," and pointed to the back door. When the dog lay down with a grunt, he told her to stay.

He led Meggie down the hallway to his bedroom where, pulling her into his arms, he fell back against the shut door and kissed her again and again, nibbling here, nipping there.

His fingers tangled in her hair. His mouth slanted across hers, lips crushing, crushing. *Meggie. At last.* Nineteen lonely years, vanished in a blink because of this. *This.*

Down her arms, his palms slid. He found the hem of her sweater, snuck beneath to warm skin. She shivered in his hands as he journeyed upward, taking the fabric with him.

For her he had waited a lifetime, a millennium, an aeon.

"Meggie," he whispered, stroking his thumbs along the curves of her flesh. "My Meggie." And then he lifted her to his waist, carried her to his bed to lay her gently down.

He would go slowly, make the moment a treasure she would remember until she was old and foggy-eyed.

He would love her as no man had loved her, tonight and every night for as long as he lived.

Tonight was the night of no return.

Tonight he would drown in her arms.

"Ethan, wait."

Her hands pressed his chest, and he rose above her, bracing himself on the heels of his palms. Gossamer moonbeams sifted through the broad window and touched the paleness of her flat tummy, her lovely breasts.

"Don't be afraid, Meggie," he murmured, when she covered her breasts. "You are woman through and through."

Below him, her chest rose and fell rapidly, her eyes held a wary glint. "Which one is it?" he asked quietly.

For a long moment she was mute, then he saw her swallow. "The left. It's not perfect. It's a little lopsided and there are scars—"

Her hand crept over the area, shielding, covering, hiding. A pang pierced his heart. After all the talk, all the explanations, the coaxing, Meggie, *his Meggie,* cop extraordinaire, was a bundle of vulnerability with him.

"Sweetheart," he began, his throat hurting from the angst he recognized in her eyes.

A cell phone played a refrain of Shania Twain's "Forever and for Always," the lyrics catchy and quick about a woman wanting to stay forever in a man's arms. A woman *determined* to keep her man forever and always.

"That's the office." She scrambled up and off the bed, tugging her sweater back into place.

Ethan rolled onto his back and sighed as he watched her grab her skirt off the floor. Vaguely he recalled unzipping the thing during their tongue and teeth dance at the bedroom door. Now she extracted the phone from a deep front pocket he hadn't known existed.

"Chief McKee.... Hi, Gilby, what's up?" Ear bent to the phone between shoulder and chin, she zipped the skirt, pushed the button through its hole. "The two of them...? Where at...? Damage to the vehicle?" She ran a hand through her hair. "Did you interview both...? Excellent.... No way.... In the trunk...? Well, isn't that interesting." She laughed lightly. "All our hard work paid off.... For sure.... No, no. That's fine. Give me ten minutes."

She flipped the phone closed, focused her attention on him. "I'm sorry, Ethan."

Tamping back frustration, he rolled off the bed. "I know, duty calls."

"Don't."

He zipped his own jeans. Had *she* unzipped him? He couldn't remember. "What's the call about?"

"Jock Ralston crashed his car into a tree out by the Blue Bull Bar and Grill. Linc Leland was with him and called his papa."

The mayor. "Are they hurt?"

"Just rattled. They've been drinking all night. Gil's got them in the tank to sober up. Hudson wants them, or at least Linc, out."

"Have you handled DUIs alone?"

"Hundreds of times." She headed for the door.

"So Gilby can't handle these on his own?"

She turned. "What're you saying?"

"That I know this is your weekend off." He walked over, touched her cheek and softened his tone. "That you're using this as an excuse to run away."

"From what?" But her gaze skipped to the bed.

"From us."

"Not at all. Gilby needs help, and I'm the only other

police person in Sweet Creek, so the responsibility falls on me."

"Hasn't he already taken their statements?"

"Yes, but—"

"Aren't they behind bars?"

"The mayor is fussing."

"Whom Gilby, a cop for six years, can't handle. That about it?"

"I'm not getting into this with you, Ethan." She turned and strode down the hallway. Thirty seconds later he heard the front door open and close…then her truck roar off into the night.

Lila's whine spurred Ethan into action. From a hook at the back door, he grabbed his jacket. "Come, old lady. Let's get some air."

Damn it, he was wrong.

She was not escaping. Nor was she hiding behind her badge to keep her clothes on with him.

This had nothing to do with self-image. She was in charge of the police department. When the mayor was involved she had to be there.

Except, he wasn't involved. Hudson hadn't done anything wrong; he'd only come to bail out his son. *So your reason for chasing back to the office on your night off is…?*

Face it, Meg. You can't walk the talk. Releasing an audible sigh, she wished she were different. *Why do you want to be so damned perfect? No one is. Not even Ethan.*

She pressed the accelerator, her heart a cyclone of confusion.

Chapter Fifteen

In his studio he worked on one of the paintings for the November show—an eagle, wings spread against a slate sky, eyes keen for movement on the rocky ledges of Blue Mountain—and thought of Meggie.

She'd been hurt by a man, emotionally scarred about her surgery. He knew it as sure as if she had told him.

I'm afraid. Oh, yeah, he understood fear. He'd hauled around a barrel of fear during those six months in prison, watching his back with every breath he took.

He wanted to slam his fist into the wall. How had she come to this point of self-deprecation and dread? Had her ex made some ridiculous remark? She'd divorced the man after her mastectomy, but who initiated the split, and more to the point, why? Because she wasn't perfect? Because someone thought she wasn't woman enough?

Yeah, he recognized self-loathing. He'd harbored it
for years as a child, a teenager and a young adult. He'd
allowed the Jock Ralstons and Linc Lelands to use that
self-loathing as a weapon, feeding on it like vultures,
bullying, pushing, taunting.

Someone, somewhere had damaged Meggie's view of
herself, and the only person she'd been with at the time
of her ordeal was Doug Sutcliffe. The mighty doctor, the
cosmetic surgeon who carved hope into an ideal.

Ethan thought about calling Beau, out at the Flying
Bar T, asking for his father's phone number. He thought
about calling Doug Sutcliffe, stripping the man of his
ego with a few choice words.

Trouble was, Sutcliffe would never accept blame for
Meggie's phobia, but that's where it had taken root. In
her marriage.

So how the hell could he defeat a process seven years
in the making? How could he heal a wound of the soul?
And how in hell could he change her self-image?

After setting his paintbrush into a tumbler of turpen-
tine, he shoved away from the drafting table. The eagle
could wait.

Outside, with Lila trotting ahead, he walked
through the night woods and let the pungency of dying leaves and grasses, and the cold, rain-scented
breeze with its hint of mountain snow, calm his un-
happy heart.

The instant Meg walked into the police station
Hudson Leland jumped from the chair in front of Sally's
reception desk. Gilby was nowhere in sight.

"This is outrageous, Chief," Hudson blustered. "Linc
shouldn't be behind bars. He didn't do anything wrong."

"He's drunk, Hudson. Once he sleeps it off, he'll be free to go. I'm sure Gilby already mentioned that."

"You're the chief. You can pull rank. Let Linc out. He can sleep it off at home with his wife or on my couch."

Meg turned to Sally. The dispatcher seldom worked weekends, but tonight she entered complaints into the system. "Where's Pearl?"

"Gone home. Gil thought I should handle—" an imperceptible nod "—things tonight."

Because of the mayor. Who received precedence—and demanded the senior police receptionist type in his son's misdeeds. Meg was familiar with the routine. Another "policy" she was beginning to loathe about her job and the Lelands. "Where's Gilby?"

"In his office writing up the report."

She walked down the corridor. Her second-in-command was at his desk, two-finger typing. She closed the door. "Hey, Gil."

"Chief."

She lowered herself to the one free chair. "Mayor giving you trouble?"

"Nah." Gilby leaned back and crossed his arms. "He wants Linc out, but I'm not releasing him until morning. Linc and I did some pushing and shoving at the scene, so he can damn well cool his heels in the slammer for a night."

"And if that doesn't work, keep him a couple days."

Gilby grinned. "You got it. By the way, did you check the bag of eagle feathers in the exhibit locker?"

The feathers found in the trunk of Jock's car. "Not yet. Jock confess?"

"It's like you suspected two weeks ago. 'Course, he claimed to know nothing." Gilby rolled his eyes. "However, when I told him he was going to jail anyway he started ranting how he needed the money and if it hadn't been for Ethan Red Wolf he'd still be manager of the rifle range." Gilby frowned. "Never was any love lost between those two, was there?"

"No." Meg remembered Ethan's expression on the bench outside the coffee shop when Jock insisted he had nothing to do with Hudson Leland hassling Ethan over the rifle range. "What about Helen's break-in?"

Gilby snorted. "A drunk man's words is a sober man's deeds, I say. Said the lock was a breeze to pick with a paper clip."

"That so?" Her mouth twitched. "Get it on tape?"

"In my notes. And that he wanted to prove a point."

She raised her brows. "A point?"

"That he's king of the hill and always will be. Jerk. Hasn't changed one damn iota since high school."

But thank God you have. "We'll see how he fares as king of the prison hill. Great work, Gil. Breakfast and lunch are on me come Monday."

His grin broadened. "Now, see—that's why I love working for you."

Something kinked in her chest as she drove through the rainy night. Gilby had handled things as well as she would have done.

Ethan had been right. She'd run.

He'd never run. Instead, he had stood his ground, battling prejudice from Jock Ralston and his ilk for nearly thirty years—and he'd survived to walk unafraid. Choosing to live in Sweet Creek where chance favored meeting the man on the street, as Ethan had two weeks ago, proved *his* point.

He had won. He had conquered.

Gripping the steering wheel as a light drizzle fell into her headlights, she felt a weight lift from her chest. He hadn't dodged the issue when she'd explained her cancer. He hadn't turned away from touching her, from longing to see *her* as she was with scars, tattoos, the *imperfection.*

Ethan was not Doug. He was not Mark.

He accepted her. He'd always accepted her. Years ago, he had understood her better than she'd understood herself, understood that their first time should be sacred and true and special, that she would've come to regret making love because of Farrah's tragedy.

"God, Meg. Seems your whole life you've picked an excuse to hide."

If she were honest, and tonight she was, she would admit her marriage had been a way to bury her unhappiness over losing the man she'd loved since she was seven years old.

Pulling into his yard, she saw the lights on in the studio and so drove toward the little building.

Her pulse raced. *Ethan* was all she could think when she shut off the motor, dug in her purse for the condoms she'd bought the previous week, climbed from the Silverado.

Raindrops wet her cheeks and dampened her hair. Intent on the glowing studio windows, she rushed forward, her tall black boots slipping on damp autumn leaves layering the path among the trees. With the onset of rain, the moon had stolen behind ragged black clouds, creating an opacity that might have chilled another. But this was Ethan's home and she was not afraid. *Never afraid.*

"Meggie." His bass voice drifted through the wet night. She spun around, searching, seeing nothing. "I'm here." Caught in the faint light from the back deck, he walked down the wooden pier.

I'm here. Oh, God, he'd always been *here.* Right here, waiting. *For her.* That she knew with every beat of her heart as she watched him quicken his pace, striding toward her, a tall figure in jeans and blue-white plaid shirt flapping open to a snowy T-shirt beneath. Ahead, the dog trotted to the back deck to seek shelter from the increasing rain.

Giddy with joy, Meg began to run.

He caught her in a tight hold, momentarily lifting her off her feet. "Forgive me," she breathed against his throat where the night, the rain intoxicated her senses. "Ethan, oh, I've been such a fool."

"Nothing to forgive, honey." Kisses on her hair, ear, eyes. "And not a fool. I love you, Meggie, so damned much. I thought I might lose you tonight. Again."

"Never." She held his dear face. Kissed his mouth. "Make love to me, Ethan. Here. Now."

He laughed softly, pushed a strand of hair from her eyes. "Have you noticed it's pouring?"

"I don't care." Tossing back her head, she reveled in the drizzle needling her cheeks and forehead. She wanted to sing, dance, shout. "I'm through waiting." She pulled his face down to hers, kissed his mouth, wrapped her arms around his neck and was lost.

"Ah, Meggie." His hands were hot on her flesh, on her belly...her breasts. And then, cupping her buttocks, he lifted her and she secured his hips with her legs, her face bent over his, kissing, oh, kissing some more.

"There," she breathed as he rotated in a slow circle in the rain. "Under the willow." It was fitting, this first mating outside in the elements he loved and prized.

A soft laugh. "You my willow woman now?" he asked, sipping raindrops from her chin.

"Now and forever."

"I like the sound of that." Against the willow, he loosened his grip and she slid down its smooth trunk. Against the willow, where they'd have some shelter from the weather. Midnight eyes a canvas of love, he thumbed her wet cheeks, the corners of her mouth.

"I brought protection." She held up the packet and he chuckled against her lips while his hands lifted her skirt, stroked her buttocks.

Rain pattered around them, on the barren branches and leaf-strewn earth, on the wooden slats of the dock, and a thrill skittered through her. They were under the tree, secreted in its sweeping branches, the two of them alone with the night and the rain. Making love for the first time. *The first time.*

"Ethan." Her fingers worked his hair, damp and scented with rain and wind and sunshine, and she gloried in the intimacy. "Ethan." Kisses, a shower of kisses.

She was glad he took the packet; now she could set her focus below his belt, on the zipper of his jeans.

"Sweetheart—" A harsh groan. "We should go in out of the rain. You must be freezing in your skirt."

"I'm burning. Please, hurry." Her fingers were inside his pants, inside his underwear where she found him heavy, ready, hot.

"Meggie." He let loose a half laugh and she heard his joy. "Go easy, babe, or this'll be over before we— *Okay.*" He hauled her hands up to his shoulders. "Hold on."

She did, and in one swift move he hiked her up against his waist, and then she was binding his hips with her legs, fastening her mouth on his, hustling her tongue inside. He tasted of wonder and mystery and Ethan. Was that moan hers—or his? Was that her heart beating against her ribs, or his? With one hand on her rump, one on her breast he pressed her against the tree's trunk, his body quivering, seeking, his mouth slanting this way, that. Urgent, urgent.

"Ethan, please." Dizzy. She was dizzy for his taste, touch, *him*.

And then, *oh!* He was *there* and she was *there,* and they gave and took and melded until all that remained was one soul.

They showered together to warm their skin and wash the weather from their hair, and before they finished, he made love to her against the tiled wall with the spray sluicing over his shoulders and her breasts, her lovely breasts.

"Can't get enough of you," he muttered, and it was true. Nineteen years he'd waited for this moment, and now that it was here, he wanted to devour her, to mainline her into his blood.

In the bathroom he patted her dry with a beach-size towel the color of her eyes, and when he was done, he held her hands, stepped back to look his fill in the light for the first time.

"The tattoos were to let them know exactly where to place the radiation machine every day," she told him, without apprehension. "The scar won't change no matter how much clobetasol I apply."

"Symbols of valor," he whispered. Reverently, he bent to kiss each tiny blue pinpoint, the line of the knife. "I'll love them always because they're part of you." His fingers tightened. "Marry me, Meggie-girl."

Tears swam in her eyes. "Oh, Ethan…"

"Is that a yes?"

"Yes and yes and yes." She shook her head. "I can't believe I walked away from you prom night."

He smiled. "Neither can I, but, hey, we wouldn't have had this night."

"We would've had it long ago," she lamented.

"Forget the past, honey, focus on the here and now."

She glanced down. A grin bloomed. "Very *here,* from what I'm seeing."

With a laugh, he caught her up and carried her to his bed.

"Mmm. I like your thinking." She caught a hank of his hair, buried her face, inhaled. "Did I tell you I'm crazy about your hair, the smell of it?"

He laid her on the quilt, climbed beside her. "You've mentioned it a time or two."

"Have you ever thought of letting it grow?"

"Like days of old?" He grinned.

"Like the man you are. I love you, Ethan." She cupped his cheeks, kissed his mouth. "And I want you on me," she whispered. "Now."

"Honey, we've done it twice in less than an hour. I don't want to make you sore."

"You won't. This is our night. I don't plan on sleeping." Her kiss was long, wet—and his blood thrummed and his heart chorused, and when he mounted her, she drove her hands into his hair and hung on.

Epilogue

June, Two Years Later

Meg followed Ethan out of the woods and into the late-afternoon sunshine. Ahead lay the boulder, symbol of their life and love. That's how Meg thought of the gigantic stone where once long ago they had vowed promises before life intruded, twisting them through a plethora of rocky years.

Today marked the twenty-first anniversary of that night when her life had spun down a separate path from Ethan's.

We've come full circle. She caught a glimpse of the boulder beyond her husband striding across the grassy shoal with their one-year-old daughter secured in a Sutemi backpack. Already Beau stood beside the rock, camera to his eye, zooming in on the mammoth eagles' nest on the ledge above.

Tears stung Meg's eyes. *Her family.* Sometimes the happiness of it all jammed its own boulder in her throat.

Two Thanksgivings ago, she and Ethan had married. Beau had led her into Ash's living room on the Flying Bar T and given her to Ethan. That winter when Meg became pregnant, she'd handed in her badge and gun and with Ethan opened Helping Horse Farm the succeeding May. She hadn't realized how much she missed working with horses until she began teaching troubled kids how to ride and care for their big gentle pets.

Best of all was the early morning arrival last July of Ariana, slipping—squalling and red-faced—into her father's strong hands and loving heart. *And so, life goes on,* Meg thought.

Ethan grinned back at her. "Come on, Mama. Beau's anxious to get the show on the road. Chandra's waiting for him to take her to the movies."

"I'm in no hurry," Beau intoned, clicking off a half-dozen shots of his baby sister. And he truly wasn't in a rush, Meg could see. Her son had come into his own, finding his path with Ethan's help and a group of new friends at college the past year.

"There you go, sprout." Ethan handed over his pink-clad daughter to her brother, who hoisted the baby onto one lean hip.

Beau pointed to the mass of twigs and branches high above. "See the eagles' nest. Up there. See, sis?"

A tiny finger poked skyward. Two dainty black pony-tails dressed in pink bows bobbed above Lilliputian ears. "Up!"

"Yep," Beau agreed. "You got it." Walking backward toward the lagoon's edge, camera raised in his other hand, Meg knew her son vied for the perfect angle.

"Now hold still, okay?" A few clicks and then he walked out of sight around the boulder. "There goes the eagle," Meg heard him murmur. "See it flying, sprout?"

Sure enough, one of the parents had levitated off the nest, flapping expansive wings in a graceful glide across the quiet waters.

Ariana's giggles floated on soft sunbeams.

Meg caught Ethan's hand. "Our daughter's entranced."

He turned those beloved dark eyes on her while a breeze fingered his shoulder-length hair. "Me, too. With you."

He could still do that, catch her at a loss for words.

When she found her voice, she said, "Think it might be our eagle?" The one he'd rescued from this spot twenty-one months before.

"Hard to say. I'd like to think it's our eagle. But if not, the fact there's a pair nesting regularly here is a very good sign."

Through the lengthening shadows, Meg looked across the lagoon. Under the vigilant eye of Blue Mountain, the terra-cotta house, her home for the past year and a half, rested like an earthen jewel amidst emerald forests.

Nesting regularly. "It's a wonderful sign," she said, and laid her cheek against her husband's shoulder.

HARLEQUIN *Romance*

New York Times bestselling author

DIANA PALMER

Handsome, eligible ranch owner Stuart York knew
Ivy Conley was too young for him, so he closed his heart
to her and sent her away—despite the fireworks between
them. Now, years later, Ivy is determined not to be
treated like a little girl anymore…but for some reason,
Stuart is always fighting her battles for her. And safe in
Stuart's arms makes Ivy feel like a woman…his woman.

Winter Roses

Available November.

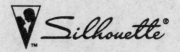

HARLEQUIN®

Mediterranean NIGHTS™

Not everything is above board
on Alexandra's Dream!

Enjoy plenty of secrets, drama and sensuality
in the latest from Mediterranean Nights.

Coming in November 2007...

BELOW DECK

by

Dorien Kelly

Determined to protect her young son,
widow Mei Lin Wang keeps him hidden
aboard *Alexandra's Dream* under cover of
her job. But life gets extremely complicated
when the ship's security officer, Gideon Dayan,
is piqued by the mystery surrounding this
beautiful, haunted woman....

HM38965

ATHENA FORCE

*Heart-pounding romance
and thrilling adventure.*

History repeats itself...unless she can stop it.

Investigative reporter Winter Archer is thrown into writing
a biography of Athena Academy's founder. But someone
out there will stop at nothing—not even murder—to
ensure that long-buried secrets remain hidden.

ATHENA FORCE

Will the women of Athena unravel Arachne's powerful
web of blackmail and death...or succumb to their
enemies' deadly secrets?

Look for

VENDETTA

by *Meredith Fletcher*

*Available November
wherever you buy books.*

Visit Silhouette Books at www.eHarlequin.com   AF38975

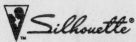

COMING NEXT MONTH

#1861 A FAMILY FOR THE HOLIDAYS—Victoria Pade
Montana Mavericks: Striking It Rich

Widow Shandie Solomon moved to Montana with her infant daughter for a new lease on life—and got one, when she opened her beauty parlor next door to Dex Traub's motorcycle shop. By Christmastime the bad boy of Thunder Canyon had Shandie hooked…and she couldn't tell if it was sleigh bells or wedding bells ringing in her future.

#1862 THE SHEIK AND THE CHRISTMAS BRIDE—
Susan Mallery
Desert Rogues

Prince As'ad of El Deharia agreed to adopt three orphaned American girls on one condition—that their teacher Kayleen James take over as nanny. In a heartbeat the young ladies turned the playboy prince's household upside down…and Kayleen turned his head. Now he would do anything to keep her—and make her his Christmas bride!

#1863 CAPTURING THE MILLIONAIRE—Marie Ferrarella
The Sons of Lily Moreau

It was a dark and stormy night…when lawyer Alain Dulac crashed his BMW into a tree, and local veterinarian Kayla McKenna came to his aid. Used to rescuing dogs and cats, Kayla didn't know what to make of this strange new animal—but his magnetism was undeniable. Did she have what it took to add this inveterate bachelor to her menagerie?

#1864 DEAR SANTA—Karen Templeton
Guys and Daughters

Investment guru Grant Braeburn had his hands full juggling stock portfolios and his feisty four-year-old daughter, Haley. So the distant widower reluctantly turned to his former wife's flighty best friend Mia Vaccaro for help. Soon Haley's Christmas list included marriage between her daddy and Mia. But would Santa deliver the goods?

#1865 THE PRINCESS AND THE COWBOY—Lois Faye Dyer
The Hunt for Cinderella

Before rancher Justin Hunt settled for a marriage of convenience that would entitle him to inherit a fortune, he went to see the estranged love of his life, Lily Spencer, one more time—and discovered he was a father. Could the owner of Princess Lily's Lingerie and the superrich cowboy overcome their volatile emotions and make love work this time?

#1866 DÉJÀ YOU—Lynda Sandoval
Return to Troublesome Gulch

When a fatal apartment blaze had firefighter Erin DeLuca seeing red over memories of her prom-night car accident that took her fiancé and unborn child years ago, ironically, it was pyrotechnics engineer Nate Walker who comforted her. At least for one night. Now, if only they could make the fireworks last longer…

SSECNM1007